A Kiss Under the Christmas Lights

by

Peggy Jaeger

A Kiss Under the Christmas Lights

COPYRIGHT © 2016 by Margaret-Mary Jaeger

Cover Art by *Rae Monet, Inc. Design*

The Wild Rose Press, Inc.
PO Box 708
Adams Basin, NY 14410-0708
Visit us at www.thewildrosepress.com

Publishing History
First Champagne Rose Edition, 2016
Digital ISBN 978-1-5092-1215-6
Print ISBN 978-1-5092-1223-1

Published in the United States of America

I swear on a stack of Bibles

and holding Nonna's rosary beads blessed by Pope Pius XII in my hands I could feel sexual tension palpating in the air.

There was no mistaking the charged energy bouncing between our bodies, though we were dressed head to toe in parkas, gloves, hats, and scarves.

I could smell it, pungent and spicy; feel it, hot and steamy; taste it, honeyed and sweet.

This is how animals must recognize their mates in the wild.

I was so glad it was dark because I knew my face looked as red as Mama's tomato sauce when it's coming to a soft boil.

Neither of us said a word. We just stared at one another. Even in the dark, I could make out the moisture flickering in his soulful eyes. His breath steamed into vapor with each expiration, a white puff of clear smoke veiling his face, and from the looks of it, he was breathing as hard and fast as I was.

My girlie parts suddenly got quite warm, the sensation not only shocking me, but exciting me as well.

Dedication

For Elvira.
You know a little sumthin' sumthin' about
large, loud, and loving Italian families.
I'm glad we are sisters-in-law.

Chapter One

"Gia Gabriella," Mama bellowed from the bottom of the staircase. *"Andiamo!* Let's go. We're gonna be late."

I cringed at the shrill sound blasting up the stairs and into my room. At just under five feet and less than a hundred pounds drenched, Mama should have a quiet, dainty little voice befitting her stature.

No such luck.

Francesca San Valentino, when she wanted or needed to, could be heard by people in New Jersey, the next state over, and even they would flinch at the deafening decibels this little Italian woman was capable of attaining.

I grabbed my down vest and shrugged into it. I was barely awake because I'd been up late into the night studying for my CPA exams and it wasn't even seven thirty yet. Forfeiting any makeup except for a small dab of concealer on the shadows under my eyes, I pulled my hair into a ponytail and barreled down the stairs of my childhood home.

Mama, hands fisted on hips that had borne six children and were still only as wide as a handspan, waited, a scowl of irritation glaring across her face only the daughter of a son of Italy can do properly.

"I'm ready to go, Mama." I stopped on the riser just above where she waited, and kissed her flawless, unlined cheek. "Don't worry. We won't be late."

"We'd better not be. I told the aunts we'd be there early to set up. And I don't want Father Mario giving me the *malocchio.*" She tossed her purse over her shoulder and made the sign of the cross in front of the current pope's picture hanging next to the front door.

As long as I could remember, there had been a photograph of the current, smiling, pious pontiff on the wall, giving us a silent wave and blessing as we left the house.

Since it was expected, I did the same.

How to be a Good Italian, Lesson 1:
Revere the Holy Father.

"Why would Fr. Mario give you the evil eye, Mama? You volunteered to help set up for the Christmas bazaar. It's not like it's expected. You're not getting paid or anything for your time."

She buckled herself into the passenger seat of her two-door compact, her suitcase-sized purse planted on her lap in front of her chest like some weird female body armor.

"Believe me, *bambina,* Fr. Mario, God bless him"—she made the sign of the cross again, her fingers dancing over the purse in the general direction of her heart, spirit, and soul—"is the type of priest who *expects* his parishioners to volunteer for church activities. If you don't, well…" One tiny shoulder pulled upward through her coat, and I couldn't see the half of her face hidden behind the fur collar. "I think he keeps a list of people who don't help out."

"Why would he?" I glided the car to a stop at a red light and glanced over at her.

She shook her head, her champagne-colored

chignon plastered in place by a lifetime's overindulgence of hairspray. "To let God know who's a good Catholic and who isn't."

I snorted a laugh. "You make the father sound like some kind of ecclesiastical Santa Claus. Who's been a naughty Catholic and who's been a nice one? That's ridiculous. I'm sure he doesn't keep a list."

Her face drew into the squinty-eyed, know-all pout every Italian mother pulls off to perfection and that basically says, "You'll see. I'm right."

The traffic was sparse on the Upper East Side of Manhattan this morning, so within ten minutes I turned into the Church of St. Rita Armada de Jesus parking lot, referred to by my four older brothers for as long as my memory could recall as *CRAP*. All four of them had been altar boys, and all four of them had hated every moment of it. Luckily, Chloe, my older sister, and I had been spared the wearing of the junior vestments because Fr. Mario was a true apostolic misogynist who believed girls should never be allowed to help serve at mass, but should be seen (if necessary) and not heard (always).

Fr. Mario was not only an old-school priest with old-school ideas, manners, and ways, he was also old as dirt. His knees clicked when he walked, the sound making anyone who heard it—and that was everyone—wince when he walked by. His ill-fitting dentures had a habit of slipping out of his mouth when he yawned, which he did often and at inappropriate times, like during the blessings at funeral masses and weddings. For the past few months, his homilies had turned from concise and predictable ten-minute sermons into rambling and repetitive twenty-five-minute tomes.

A few nights ago at dinner, Daddy mentioned he'd

heard from a guy who knew the bishop that a new priest, fresh out of seminary and not even ordained yet, had been assigned to St. Rita's to assist the aging Fr. Mario.

In everyone's opinion, the new guy couldn't arrive soon enough.

This morning, the back half of the church parking lot was roped off and filled with makeshift wooden huts that would serve as the individual booths for the upcoming holiday celebration.

Every year, St. Rita's hosts a countdown-to-Christmas festival during the twelve days before the holiday, culminating in a Christmas Eve vigil at the church with a program of Mary and Joseph's trek into Bethlehem acted by local parish kids.

"The new guy is supposed to be here this morning, helping out," Mama said as I parked the car.

"What's his name?" I buttoned up my vest against the biting cold rolling off the East River and cursed myself for not dressing warmer.

"Fr. Santini."

"You're kidding? His name literally means *little saint*, and he's a priest?"

Mama is a walking encyclopedia of kinesthesia and can relay a simple or a complex idea with just a few easy movements of her body. So when she turned to me, lifted her shoulders, palms upward at her waist, and pouted again, closing her crystal-blue eyes and raising her pencil-thin eyebrows almost to her hairline, I knew she was telling me, in essence, "What can you say?"

From the trunk of the car, I helped Mama remove our contribution to the festival: Christmas lights for the booths. Strand after strand of tiny bright white lights would be strung over, across, and down the huts to illuminate them to the holiday hordes who attended the festival each year.

You know those tiny clown cars in the circus you think fit two clowns, but when the car door opens, about twenty come barreling out one after the other? Just like those cars, every time I pulled another bag filled with light boxes out of the trunk, more would materialize.

"*Gesu*, Mama," I said, lifting a bunch of bags from the trunk. "How many did you buy?"

"I figured ten boxes of one hundred lights per booth would do it."

I did a quick mental calculation—CPA candidate, remember? "There are fifteen huts, so you bought one hundred and fifty boxes?"

She nodded, wrapping three plastic bag handles around one hand.

"That's fifteen thousand lights. How much did all that cost?"

"Not much." Her chin disappeared behind her fur collar again when she lifted a shoulder. "Your uncle Sonny knew a guy, so I got a good deal."

Uncle Sonny, my dad's younger brother by ten months and five days (hey, we're Italian Catholics, so what can I say?) is what is called in polite circles *connected*. In our house that means he intimately knows people who can get you anything you want, from whatever make and model car you desire to helping you get rid of a pain-in-the-neck in-law.

And when I say *get rid of,* I mean it in the literal sense of the word.

You never saw them again.

Ever.

"The aunts are bringing extension cords," Mama

told me as she started dropping off bags of light boxes at each hut.

After an hour of helping people move supplies from cars, I passed by Mama, who was carrying a humongous swaddled baby Jesus statue for the crèche.

"The new guy is here," she called out.

"Where?" I put down the ladder I'd been carting and looked in the general direction of where she'd cocked her chin since her arms were full of the Lord.

I found him in an instant. It wasn't difficult because he was the only guy in the parking lot I didn't recognize. Plus, he was dressed head to toe in basic clergy wear: black long-sleeved shirt under a black vest over black trousers and standard-issue shiny black, boring priest shoes.

His back was to me and he was carrying a table, but after he put it down and turned around, I got a good look at the front of him.

And *Holy Mary, Mother of God,* what a front he had.

Close-cropped, military-style hair the color of windblown wheat topped a head that stood—truly—head and shoulders above everyone else around. The guy had to be six three at least. Sharp, etched cheekbones God cut with a knife sat under deep and dark oval-shaped eyes. His face was a composite of planes and angles, the carved cheeks meeting up with a chiseled-from-stone chin. Hardened concrete looked softer than this guy's jawline. His nose was perfectly fixed in the center of his face, the slight aquiline bend at the tip bringing to mind Michelangelo's David, the Cupid's bow under it well defined and pronounced. His lips were full and thick and—God help me—looked utterly kissable.

I could tell even with the chunky vest covering his torso, he was closer to thin than stocky, but from the way his biceps pulled against his sleeves, he had some muscle to him.

And some pair of legs. They went on forever, from heaven to earth in a full, hard line.

I don't know how long I stood there just gawking with my mouth open like an empty cannoli shell waiting to be filled, but I'm being truthful when I say I couldn't move. My feet were frozen to the ground, my knees had locked, and my hips weren't taking me anywhere soon.

This was one beautiful man.

The old masters would have used him as a springboard for their work, and I could actually picture him in a Botticelli fresco, garbed in Roman robes, lounging while naked, buxom-breasted chubby women fed him grapes and sweetmeats.

In the time it took for a hummingbird to flap its wings once, I pictured myself as one of those women.

Just when it hit me this was my new parish priest— a priest, for pity's sake—he turned, and our gazes locked across the lot.

His dark eyes widened, and his beautiful full mouth opened, forming the sexiest *O* I'd ever seen on a guy. With a slow, steady determination, he stood to his full height, shoulders folding back and squaring, his neck doing a little stretchy thing that sent my stomach muscles into a conniption fit.

Unlike me, he could move. And did.

Straight across the parking lot and straight to me.

Madonna!

As he came toward me, I could see every ripple of

7

muscle, every action and reaction of his gait, every blink of his eyes while it happened. Detailed, distinct, delicious.

The bright sun shone low due to the hour, but it haloed around his form, bathing him in light.

He looked like an angel. A dressed-all-in-black angel, but an angel, nonetheless.

"Need some help?" he asked when he was within a foot of me.

I still hadn't moved, my fingers cemented around the ladder rungs. I couldn't feel them anymore. *Merda,* I couldn't feel anything I was so numb from just looking at him.

But I could hear. My blood, as it river-rafted crazily through my temples; my heart, drumming like a heavy metal band in my chest.

And his voice. *Mio Dio,* his voice.

When I was six, I'd had a terrible chest cold. The doctor told Mama to keep me warm and hydrated and the cold would ride itself out in time. Nonna prescribed her own old-world remedy. She sat me in her lap and held a tiny shot glass up to my lips coaxing, *"Tu bevi, Gia bambina. Tu bevi."* Drink, Gia baby. Drink.

She tilted the glass back into my mouth, and I drank every drop.

I don't remember much after because Daddy told me I slipped into a coma for about sixty hours, bombed out of my head from the anisette Nonna dosed me with.

But what I do remember is the amber-colored liquid slipping to the back of my throat, warming each place it touched like a million little hits of heat popping everywhere inside me and filling my senses with the sweet flavor of Mama's Sunday morning caramel rolls and sugar.

That's what his voice sounded like: warm and sweet, thick, delicious, and soothing.

My entire body relaxed when I heard it. My paralysis flew, and my frozen-in-place digits melted.

He'd held my stare the entire time, never wavering, never becoming distracted by something else. He looked straight at me, like a missile deadeye-aimed for a target.

"This looks heavy," he said as he finagled the ladder out of my grip. "Where do you want it?"

With as much effort as it would have taken me to lift a feather, he raised the heavy ladder on to his shoulder.

"Um?"

Really? This was the best I could do? I shook the dust bunnies out of my head and pointed. "Over by those wooden huts."

"After you," he said in the voice that had my legs— and all my other necessary parts—liquefying.

We walked over to the first hut, which belonged to the St. Rita's convent, the nuns big hawkers of their own handmade Christmas cards.

We stopped, and he opened the ladder. "Is this a good spot?"

I was struck mute again when I glanced up at his face. And I *did* have to glance up. Way up.

I'm blessed with Mama's DNA, unlike my brothers and sister who favor my tall, swarthy, Mediterranean-gened dad. I was their opposite in every way: small-boned, blonde, and blue-eyed northern Italian genes flow through me, which include a genetic marker for short stature. If I stood completely upright without a bend or kink in my spine, I could manage five foot three.

So when I say I had to curve back in order to see his face in full, I'm not exaggerating.

"Perfect. Thanks."

"I'm Tim Santini, by the way." He stuck out his hand, and I stared down at it for a few beats. "My friends call me T."

A cute nickname, but I wasn't a friend so there was no way I was calling him by an initial. "Tim" seemed too informal since he was a priest and I'd been raised to respect the calling and the called, so I opted to graze over any moniker and simply said, "Gia San Valentino. My friends call me Gia."

He chuckled as I slipped my hand into his.

And time stopped.

I know it sounds hokey and clichéd, and maybe it is. But truly, everything around us slowed, stilled.

A moment ago the parking lot had been filled with people, all talking, gossiping, working, and the noise level had been what you'd expect from a crowd.

But the moment I folded my hand into his, all sound ceased.

A confused little stutter shifted in his gorgeous eyes, and I knew exactly how he felt.

I pulled my hand from his with just a little too much force and took a step backward, mentally and physically. "I've got to get these lights strung." I reached for one of Mama's numerous boxed sets and started opening it. "Thanks for helping with the ladder."

I figured he'd go on to help the next person who needed assistance, but he didn't. He stayed with me while I began opening the light boxes. For some ridiculous reason, though, my hands weren't working and I couldn't get the first box open. The flap was taped shut on both ends with what had to be industrial-strength adhesive mixed with superglue because no matter how hard I tugged and yanked, I couldn't split it.

Frustration and nerves got the better of me. *"Gesu!* Stupid tape," I said before I could stop myself.

In the next nanosecond, my cheeks burned with fire. My head snapped up to see Santini watching me struggle, his hunky arms crossed in front of his chest, a closed-mouth grin lurking on his lips.

"I'm so sorry," I said on a gasp, my hands practically crushing the box between them.

Great way to make an impression on the new priest, Gia. Take the Lord's name in vain.

"Forgive me, please, I—"

"You're forgiven. Give it over." He put a hand out for the box.

My hand visibly shook as he took it from me.

He pulled a Swiss Army knife from the back pocket of his trousers, and with one flick to open it and another to slice the tape, the problem was solved.

"How many of these do you have?" He opened the flap and pulled out the plastic container housing the crammed rows of light strings.

"A hundred and fifty boxes." I swallowed. Hard.

"Did you get them all at the same store?"

He handed the tray to me and picked up another box of lights, slicing and dicing it as he had the first one.

"My mother got them, and I don't think she went to a store. My uncle, um, well, he…knows a guy…you know…who kind of gave her a…um…deal."

Nothing like confessing to your new spiritual advisor your family communes with shady people who get you things that fell off a truck to make you feel even more unworthy and destined for hell.

For some reason, Santini didn't appear to think this was an issue. He didn't even bat an eyelash, just kept on cutting open boxes.

"Do you know how you want to string them up?" he asked as he worked.

"Along the top of each hut and then down the sides, to illuminate the frames. Extension cords will connect each individual strand together, forming one long electrical strip per hut."

"Good idea." He stopped slicing and graced me with a bountiful smile. "You won't need a bunch of adaptors for every booth, then."

I nodded. "That's what my mama was thinking."

I swear his smile could have paved the way to heaven through the darkness with its sheen and brilliance.

"Here," he said when he'd gotten the first five or so boxes opened. "Why don't I hand them up, and you string them? You're way smaller and lighter than I am. Your ladder"—he pointed his chin at it—"doesn't look like it would hold me."

I nodded and climbed up. Even though I was almost on the top rung, I still wasn't taller than he was.

But we were eye to eye, and when I tell you how amazing it was to be level with his handsome face, believe me, it was. I could make out the actual color of his eyes now. I'd thought they were dark from far away, but seeing them face to face, I spotted little flecks of yellow and slivery shards of gold mixed into the center and surrounded by a ring of deep, rich mink.

If his voice was warm and soothing, his eyes were hot enough to singe, and *mama mia*, I wanted to be burned.

I had to give myself a mental reminder about why I was standing here. It was so I could string lights, not stare with unbridled pleasure at a guy who was the physical embodiment of the term "eye candy."

But, *mio Dio*, did I want to do just that.

Chapter Two

We hammered out a good rhythm between us, with Santini passing the lights up and me attaching them to the wooden frame of the hut and then connecting each string to the next one to form one continuous light strand.

Since the bazaar was open twelve hours a day for the twelve days preceding Christmas and we were now ensconced in full-fledged standard time, where we'd turned the clocks back an hour so it wouldn't be as dark as death when we all got up in the morning and the kids didn't have to wait at the bus stop with flashlights, night routinely descended around four every afternoon. The parking lot lights were all on automatic timers to save the diocese money and didn't click on until almost seven, so that meant three hours of the daily festival would be celebrated in the dark unless we lit the huts.

The diocese lawyers, always afraid of a slip-and-fall negligence lawsuit, had demanded that if we put up huts, we put up lights to go with them.

So here we were.

"This is quite a volunteer turnout," he said. "I'm impressed."

"The St. Rita's Christmas Festival is a neighborhood favorite," I told him as I secured the first string around the plastic holder along the top of the hut. "People from all over the parish and the neighborhood come and sell stuff, donating a portion of their sales back to the church."

He asked me a bunch of questions about how volunteers were procured, who was in charge of the event, how we did takedown when it was over. All things he would need to know since he was now second in command of the parish.

Santini was very easy to talk to, something I guess in his profession was an asset, and once I got over how unbelievably good-looking he was, I found myself relaxing and answering all his questions minus the nerves.

At one point he asked, "Where are the extension cords you need?"

The second the words left his lips, a horn honked from the lot entrance, and a big-ass classic model Caddy zipped in, a car I knew belonged to my aunt Gracie, Mama's older sister.

The car pulled to a metal-scraping halt, just missing the concrete parking divider. The chassis ping-ponged front, then back, twice, from the force of the brake, and the metallic grating sound of the gear shifter being thrown into the park position before the car completely stopped was audible from where I stood fifty feet away. I said a silent prayer to St. Christopher, the patron saint of travelers, to protect the aunts from harm while driving.

And to protect all other drivers from my aunts.

Aunt Gracie alighted from the car, an electronic cigarette dangling from her *Cherries in the Snow* lipstick-covered mouth, and adjusted her bra strap. She tugged from an area almost waist level, and I watched in horror (as I had ever since the first time I'd been scarred for life by seeing her do this at the age of seven) as she hauled her bowling-ball-sized breasts back into place on her chest. With a final shove up of each mound from under her ribcage, she waved to us and went to the passenger door to help Mama's other sister, Nicoletta, my aunt Nicci, out.

The reason Nicci needed help getting out of the car was a bit of a family mystery. She was the youngest of the sisters at just fifty-eight, but whenever I asked my mother why her sister couldn't get out of a car on her own or go up or down stairs without holding someone's hand, I was always met with Mama quickly crossing herself and mumbling something about black cats, birth defects, and *il Diavolo.*

Crazy family, much?

How to be a good Italian, Lesson Two:
Don't ask and never tell. Ever.

Have you ever wanted the ground to open up and just swallow you whole? Then you can sympathize with the flood of embarrassment washing through me at that moment.

"Ah"—I felt my face turn sixteen shades of boiled-tomato red—"there they are now. Those are two of my aunts, and they've got the cords with them."

"You stay," he said when I started to come down the ladder. "I'll go get them."

Truthfully, I didn't want him anywhere near those two, but for such a big guy, he moved like a lightning flash.

From my vantage point, I watched while he smiled at them and then took a box Aunt Gracie pulled out of her trunk. With a quick wave over his shoulder, he came back to me, and the aunts went off, most likely in search of my mother.

"Thanks," I said when he took the connected string I'd made and attached it to one of the cords.

"Your aunts remind me of my own," he said, a tiny, knowing smile tripping across his lips.

"Oh? Are they loud and inappropriate like mine are?"

I swear, his laugh could make the minions of hell smile.

"Something like that," he said after we'd finished the nun hut and moved on to the next one. "So, Gia San Valentino, have you been a parishioner of St. Rita's for long?"

"Life-long member," I said. "I was baptized, communed, confirmed, and reconciled here. All by Fr. Mario."

"Four sacraments in one church. That's impressive. All you're missing are holy orders, marriage, and extreme unction for the ultimate win in the Catholicism sweepstakes."

I laughed.

"I was even the baby Jesus once during the parish Christmas vigil," I told him.

I explained that every year the festival culminated in a Christmas Eve vigil at the church with a program of Mary and Joseph's trek into Bethlehem acted by local parish kids. I'd been the baby Jesus one year since there hadn't been any infant boys available.

Fr. Mario had been a tad, shall we say, *pissed* at a girl playing the role of our Lord and Savior. He had to suck it up, though, because the next youngest boy baby in the parish had been Luca Provincioni, who was two and half, a lover of all things pasta, and already tipped

17

the scales at forty-eight pounds. There was no way the parishioners would buy having a toddler—and one almost as large as the Virgin Mary-playing kid—portray the baby Jesus. So Mama had volunteered me for the role.

Daddy keeps a picture of me swaddled and looking angelic in his wallet to this day.

A low whistle blew from Santini's downright marvelous mouth, and for half a second, I stopped stringing just to bask in it. When it lifted into a grin just too divine and mischievous to be considered proper for a priest, he added, "The ultimate starring role."

I grinned at the laughter in his voice.

"My acting debut and my final curtain call all in one night," I said.

"A brilliant, but short-lived career. The entertainment world doesn't know what it missed."

I was charmed and utterly bedazzled by him. He was so— *Normal* is the only word I can think of. Not like the stuffy, grumpy old priest I'd been exposed to my entire life. Fr. Mario would never, ever, have made a joke about our religion—even a simple, innocuous one.

"So, what about those remaining sacraments?" he asked.

"Well..." I came down the ladder to move it to the next spot I needed to string. "I'm not knocking at death's door, so last rites aren't in order, and I have no intention of becoming a nun, much to my *nonna's* every-waking-hour regret."

He laughed again, and the sound settled in my stomach like warm amaretto custard.

"So that just leaves marriage," he said.

I adjusted the ladder where I wanted it and turned to

look up at him, hearing a strange chord in his voice.

Something on his face, in his eyes, caused my insides to go a little wonky, like the feeling I'd had after my first-ever glass of champagne at my brother Gianni's wedding where I was the flower girl. A little fluttery, a little tingly, a little unexpected shot of warmth all competing for domination.

"So"—his eyes focused on mine, a glimmer of what looked to me like expectation in them—"any plans for that one? Anyone you're presently planning to commit to for eternity?"

If I didn't know he was almost a priest, a man of the cloth, a soldier of God Almighty, I would have sworn on a boulder stacked high with Bibles he was flirting with me.

But he *was* a priest, so there was no way he was. He was just being friendly and priest-nosy. After all, weddings and funerals are his bread and butter.

"If that's your way of asking if I'm engaged, the answer is no." I climbed back up the ladder. "No boyfriend at present, no plans to marry in the near future. I've been busy with school. Not much time for anything else. In fact, I should be home studying right now, but my mother...well. When you get to know her, you'll see. No one says no to her when she asks you to do something. Probably because she doesn't ask. She tells."

I reached down to take the string of lights he was handing up.

"But someday, right?" he asked. "You'll want to get married? Have children?"

"Sure. Isn't marriage and motherhood the hope and dream of every little Italian girl?" I secured the lights around the plastic holder. "And their mothers?" I glanced down at him. "And grandmothers?"

His laugh was quick and free and punched me in the stomach like a cheap shot. I stopped stringing just to stare at his holy hotness. And I mean that in the best ecclesiastical sense.

"And their aunts and sisters?" he added, squinting up at me, the sun in his face, a smile across it. "Uncles and brothers?"

"First cousins and best friends?" I laughed along with him. This was more fun than I'd had in a while, or in my entire life of dealing with Fr. Mario. This is the way a priest should be. Outgoing, fun, and friendly. Not stuffy, sanctimonious, and self-righteous.

Happy, enthusiastic, and sweet.

And good-looking. Good-looking didn't hurt at all. The kind of guy you'd love to date, have pay you attention, make out with.

Reality washed through me in that instant. The same blinding paralysis I'd suffered earlier sluiced down my body, making movement impossible.

All the blood shunted to my brain.

Holy Mary, Mother of God!

Of all the people in the world to think about making out with, I had to pick my new pastor.

Nonna's voice barked in my head. *Muto*, Gia. Dumb. *Stupido ragazza*! Stupid girl.

I *was* stupid. Not to mention if my mother ever found out I was having carnal—okay, mildly carnal, not full-fledged—thoughts about a man of the cloth, she would pinch my ears between her fingers, drag me straight to St. Rita's convent, sign me in, and under my name list the word *puttana*. Whore.

He must have noticed I wasn't moving because Santini reached over and laid a hand on my upper arm. "Gia? You okay?"

The heat seeping through his hand, through my jacket, through my skin, pulled me out of my immobility.

"Yeah. Yeah, I'm okay."

"You went somewhere else for a second."

Before thinking I was about to commit a sin to a man of God, mortification got the better of me and I lied. "I'm just hungry. I didn't have a chance to eat this morning before we got here."

If he'd known my mother personally, he would have known this for the bald-faced lie it was. Not one of her children, grandchildren, relatives, or friends ever left Francesca San Valentino's house hungry.

Ever.

For a moment, I got lost in the way he was staring at me and in how good his hand felt, still on my arm. Something passed in his eyes as he looked at me, like he'd had a deep, mind-blowing epiphany.

I stood, mesmerized, as the darker circles around his irises widened, dilating so much the lighter colors broke free. His tongue ran across his lips in an unconscious trail—*Holy mother of God, save me!*—and his neck bobbled up and down as he swallowed a few times.

I don't think I've ever been looked at quite the way he was looking at me. Equal parts of confusion and puzzlement mated with heat and, God forgive me, *passion.*

At least I think it was passion. It could have been repulsion, for all I knew. Or gas.

He was still holding my arm, his thumb rubbing in

little circular motions over the sleeve of my shirt. The breeze billowing off the East River picked up, and the fringe on top of his head blew forward across his forehead. It took every ounce of willpower I still had inside me not to reach out and push those hairs back in place. For a millisecond, the image of Barbara Streisand doing that to Robert Redford in *The Way We Were* (Mama's favorite movie) shot across my eyes.

Little electrical flashes burst along my insides, and I pressed my thighs together when they started to shake, a totally insane move since the heat erupting in that region was scorching.

I think I moaned.

Gesu, Gia. Get a grip.

Santini licked his delicious-looking lips again, his eyes staying glued to mine, and said, "Look, why don't we—" before he was cut off by the sound of a ringtone.

He let go of my arm and reached around to his back pants pocket to pull out a cell phone. A quick glance at the display screen caused a groove to pop up on his forehead, his kissable lips bending downward at the corners.

His thumbs hit the keypad a few times, and then he turned his attention back to me.

I was still standing, rooted to the ladder.

"Gia, I'm sorry. I've got a work crisis. I've gotta go."

"No worries," I said automatically. "You have a lot of responsibility in your position."

The groove across his brow deepened. "I…" He stopped short again, the confusion on his face growing. "It was great meeting you. Talking with you."

"Likewise." I tried to summon a smile.

I think it came out looking more like the face Nonna makes when she needs a laxative.

He nodded, reached out, and squeezed my upper arm again.

"See you around."

"Yeah." I swallowed the bocce ball in my throat. "See you in church."

He squinted at me for half a second, then nodded and walked to the other side of the parking lot, so packed with volunteers I lost sight of him almost at once.

What in the name of God and family was wrong with me?

My hands started to tremble, the light strand in them jiggling underneath my quaking. I was afraid I'd topple off the ladder since my knees had turned to powder, so I grabbed hold of the sidebars and carefully made my way down to the ground again, one slow rung at a time.

My breathing was a little shallow, a little fast, a little unsteady.

And my mind was a whole lot of confused.

Chapter Three

"You're not eating, *bambina*," Mama said. "What's wrong?"

We were all seated, and by *we* I mean the whole family—my brothers, their wives and kids; my sister, her husband, son, and my new baby niece; Mama, Daddy, Nonna; Uncle Sonny and his wife, Aunt Ursula; Aunts Gracie and Nicci and their husbands—all around our huge dining-room table, having dinner later that night.

"Nothing's wrong, Mama," I said as every adult eye at the table impaled me and then assessed my plate with squinty-eyed stares.

It is always assumed in an Italian family if you are not eating you are either sick, worried, or dying.

I'm not kidding.

"I'm just tired from studying and then being outdoors all morning in the cold air."

"I told you she wasn't dressed warm enough, Frankie," Aunt Gracie said. She scraped a fingernail along something stuck in one of her top teeth. She got it out, examined it, and then stuck her finger back in her mouth, chowing down on whatever little morsel it had been.

"You need to eat, baby." Daddy reached over and grabbed my hand. "You need to get those brain cells all pumped up for your exam on Monday."

"I know, Daddy. Don't worry, I'll be fine."

"Gia, I know a guy who's looking for a numbers person," Uncle Sonny said. "A new business venture he's putting together on the Lower West Side. One of those trendy cybercafes. Frou-frou coffees with names no one can pronounce, big-ass muffins and breads and stuff. He could use someone with a math brain like yours to help him with the books and the spreadsheets. I could put a good word in his ear for ya."

He was seated across the table from me, his bright blue suspenders sitting over his old-as-sin, used-to-be-white, wife-beater tee. The only time Uncle Sonny ever wore an actual shirt was when he left the house. Any time he was inside, no matter whose house it was—his own or someone else's—he removed his dress shirt, electing to be comfortable in his undershirt and pants. The suspenders were a necessary item, not a sartorial statement, because he'd gained some substantial weight in the past few years and hated the wincing feeling of a belt around his ever-expanding waistline. His pants hung underneath his bulging abdomen and would have fallen to the floor if not anchored by the suspenders.

Before I could respond, Mama beat me to it.

"Salvador San Valentino." Her voice rose to a pitch that could summon dogs. "You will not give my *bambina*'s name to any of your wise-guy friends, do I make myself clear?"

"Frankie, honey," Sonny said, all sweetness and light oozing from his voice, a smile Nonna always termed *oily* across his mouth. "No worries. This guy's legit."

"No one you know is legit," she shot back, rising and moving around the table with the filled pasta bowl to give refills.

She slapped a wooden spoon the size of a cup measure onto my brother Gianni's plate with a *thwack.* "It's bad enough everything you own fell off a truck." She moved onto my youngest brother, Edoardo's plate. *Thwack.* "And that you associate with people on police wanted lists." On to Antonio. Another *thwack.* "But you're Joey's brother, so I overlook all that." *Thwack* onto Nonna's plate—although she hadn't eaten any of her first pasta round yet. "But I draw the line when you want to involve my baby girl in the businesses of your low-life, crooked friends."

With a final *thwack* to Daddy's plate, she slammed the bowl, which was almost as wide as she was, back onto the table and picked up the gravy boat.

"Who wants sauce?" she snapped, her crystal-blue gaze flitting with anger around the table.

"Here, Mama." Chloe's husband, Matt, stood and took the antique piece of imported Italian china from her. "I'll do it. You sit. Eat. You must be tired from working at the church all day and then making this wonderful meal for us all."

Gently, he nudged the gravy bowl from her hands, charming her with his dashing smile and melted-chocolate-colored eyes.

Unable to resist smiling back at him—he was after all the golden son-in-law since he was a doctor and had given her two more grandchildren to fawn over—Mama patted his cheeks. "You're such a good boy, Matteo. I'm so happy my Chloe married you."

From next to me, I heard my brother Paolo mutter, "Suck up," and I choked a laugh into my napkin.

"Did you get a glance at the new guy today?"

Daddy asked Mama, diverting her wrath away from his brother.

"What a looker." She lifted her wineglass to her lips. "He's got a face that should be in the movies, not in a pulpit, right, Gia baby?"

"You met him?" my sister Chloe asked as she held her new daughter, Arianna. "Is he nice?"

I nodded and shoved a forkful of pasta in my mouth and prayed I wasn't blushing.

"He was very helpful to the volunteers." Mama spooned some fresh grated parmigiana cheese over her pasta. "But he couldn't stay long. Fr. Mario called him back to the rectory. Something about the bishop's upcoming visit. But he's a looker, all right."

I could feel the heat rising up my neck. I took a huge chug of my own wine.

"He's saying the nine o'clock mass in the morning," Mama told the table. "We'll leave at the usual time."

By that she meant we had all better be ready by eight thirty to march out the door *in famiglia.*

This family did everything important together: eat, live, die, attend church.

Sometimes living in such a close-knit family is a little bit suffocating and a whole lot of claustrophobic.

How to be a Good Italian, Lesson 3:
Family comes first, last, forever,
and you do everything together. Always.

"Gia," Chloe said, breaking into my thoughts. "Come and help me with your goddaughter. She needs to be changed."

She rose and grabbed the diaper bag sitting in the living room with one hand, her other hand holding her two-month-old. "Lorenzo, be a good boy for Nonna and

Papa," she told her two-year-old son with a kiss to his head.

Up in Gianni and Paolo's old bedroom, which now served as an all-things-*bambino* warehouse, Chloe held the baby up to me and said, "Here. You do the honors." Once she handed her over, she plopped down into the rocking chair Mama had rocked all six of us in and let out a sigh that tugged at my heart.

I laid Arianna down on the changing table Nonna had brought over from Italy with her seventy-five years ago, and tickled her little belly. Her toothless grin stared up at me. She was already a heartbreaker and owned my own heart and soul completely.

"Okay, baby sister." Chloe folded her hands across her stomach. "Spill. What's up?"

"What do you mean?" I popped open the crotch of the onesie, pushed it up to Arianna's tiny waist, and bent down to kiss her soft, swollen, little baby belly.

"Your face went the color of Mama's sauce when they started discussing the new priest. What gives?"

Chloe is nine years older than I am and one of the smartest women I know. At times she's been more of a mother to me than our own, like during the horrible two years Mama went through chemo treatments for breast cancer when I was eleven. Chloe was the one who helped me buy my first bra, taught me about my period, and listened to me when I had questions about boys, sex, and what constituted appropriate dating behavior for girls who came from families like ours: overprotected.

I could talk to her about anything. Anything, except this. There was no way I could explain the way I'd reacted to Santini. No way I could confess I had the hots for an almost-priest. No way I could say the words out loud that would brand me a *puttana*.

I changed Arianna's diaper and told Chloe I was tired from studying and stressing about my upcoming exams.

"I wanted to sleep in today, but Mama yelled me out of bed at seven."

Chloe chuckled. "I remember those days when she used to do that to get us all up for school. I swore she was the alarm clock for every kid on our street."

"No lie. I could have slept 'til noon. I'm just supertired, and I can't wait until this whole exam session is over."

I could tell she didn't quite believe my excuse, but that's the wonderful thing about Chloe. Unlike our mother, who vigorously browbeats and badgers you like a Vegas mob boss until you can't stand it anymore and you wind up confessing to things you didn't even do, Chloe doesn't push.

I picked up my goddaughter, gave her a slew of kisses across her cheeks, and handed her back to her mother.

Later on, when everyone who didn't live in my parents' home anymore left for their own houses, I lay in my bed, my exam prep book open on my lap, staring up at the wooden crucifix on my wall.

I said a silent prayer the next time I met the good father I would be able to act normally and not like a middle-school girl with an adolescent crush on the new, hot teacher.

****

After another sleep-deprived night, I was in the back seat of Daddy's classic Buick sitting next to Nonna, on our way to St. Rita's.

"The new guy's doing mass by himself," Mama said from the front seat as she checked herself in the car's mirror. "I heard it from Dottie Allegari yesterday, who heard about it at choir practice."

My insides did a fast little jig, and I regretted eating the second helping of sausage Mama had shoved on my plate for breakfast. Outwardly, I tried to appear calm.

Daddy parked, and I was in charge of helping Nonna get out of the car and into the church without falling and—God forbid—breaking a hip. A serious fall was a daily worry for the family as Nonna shuffled around my parents' house, always dusting, straightening, or cleaning something, whether it needed it or not.

Mama and the aunts had talked recently in hushed voices about possibly putting Nonna in the nursing home where her brother Vito lived, but she heard them whispering and screeched in Italian she would put a curse on them all and their families if they did.

Ninety-three years old, and she still hears like a bat.

Chloe and her family were seated in our family pew. We greeted them with kisses and hugs like we hadn't seen them for decades instead of just last evening, and I immediately grabbed my goddaughter. She was sleeping soundly and looked like one of Botticelli's cherubs: chubby, pink cheeked, and bow lipped. I was so in love with this little *bambina*, there were days I just wanted to steal her away from my sister.

The organ struck a chord, signaling the "all rise," which we did, and the choir began singing.

St. Rita's is an old church dating back to before the First World War. Befitting the architecture of the day, it has a huge domed ceiling, and the altar is a plaster fresco of carved doves and angels surrounding the communion table. Stained-glass windows depicting Christ's march to crucifixion border two walls, a marble walkway from the back of the church to the front running up the middle.

Since Christmas was a little over two weeks away, the Ladies' Altar Society had bedecked the church in splendor. Several eight-foot fir trees surrounded the outer perimeter of the altar, each filled with hundreds of white, sparkling lights. For a hot second, I wondered if the head of the society knew Uncle Sonny's "light guy."

Dozens of cardinal-red poinsettia plants, just coming into bloom, sat along the sides of the steps leading up to the altar and were scattered around the priests' chairs.

The lit Advent candle was positioned off to one side of the lectern, two of the four candles blazing brightly. Yards and yards of fresh boxwood were strung along the beginning of each pew, making the church smell like a Christmas tree farm. In all, the ladies had done an outstanding job. It truly felt like Christmas.

While I held and rocked a sleeping Arianna, the choir sang their little hearts out and the procession up the aisle began.

First, the standard bearer, holding the six-foot golden crucifix, a task my father had done until his heart attack a few years ago had left him too weak to lift the heavy, solid cross.

Next, the lector holding the Bible in an act of reverence above her head. When I was younger, my brother Paolo had been grounded for a month when he made me burst out laughing by saying as the lector went by, "Stick 'em up, lady!"

Mama had gently cuffed him on the back of the head, while Nonna flicked a finger to his temple, both of them saying at the same time, "What is wrong with you? You're in church, for God's sake. A little respect," and then crossing themselves.

They totally missed they'd been disrespectful by taking the Lord's name in vain, but hey, I wasn't going to tell them and risk a head ticking of my own.

Two middle-school-aged altar servers decked out in black cassocks with white shoulder capes came after the lector, looking sleepy and bored, much the way I imagined my brothers routinely looked when they'd done this job.

Next and last came Fr. Santini.

I'd lain in bed wondering if seeing him was going to affect me the same way it had the day before. Would my pulse go all wonky and erratic again? Would I feel like I was fighting for air? Would the area at the top of my thighs shake with—God forgive me—need?

Fr. Santini smiled at Mama, and then his gaze drifted to Arianna and finally up to mine, and…nothing. Not one bit of the mind-numbing lust I'd experienced yesterday shot through me today. My mind processed he was still gorgeous, even more so in his resplendent vestments, but that was all. No toe curling, no leg shaking, no heart pounding. *Niente*. Nothing.

He hadn't acknowledged me, hadn't raised an eyebrow in recognition, or smiled a little wider. He just kept singing and walking.

Well.

For the first time in over twenty-four hours, I relaxed, chalking yesterday's unusual out-of-control emotions up to lack of sleep and test anxiety, much as

I'd told Chloe the night before.

The congregation sat when instructed, and the mass began.

Just before Fr. Santini was about to speak the Gospel and give his homily, Arianna began to fuss and squirm. I tried to calm her by cooing and rubbing her back, but she'd have none of it. Her tiny, chubby little hands were balled into fists, her beautiful bow-shaped mouth pouted and pulled in all directions, her face a little mask of torment. Just as her body straightened and arched, her little fists standing upright as if ready to do battle, I heard Chloe suck in a breath and then a rumble and a gurgling noise so loud several people in pews around us turned toward it.

Before I realized what was going to happen, Arianna pulled a full-body shudder, and a humongous explosion filled with the unmistakable aroma of fresh baby poop shot from her. The air around us instantly turned toxic, and the diaper secured to Arianna's tiny baby butt suddenly grew watery and warm through her bunting.

"Rianna pooped," Lorenzo declared to one and all in his outside—not inside—voice.

Chloe wrapped a hand around his mouth as he started to giggle with adorable two-year-old glee. Nonna shot steel daggers from her rheumy eyes at him, and before she could tap him on his head, Chloe dragged him onto her lap, ever the protective mama lioness.

"You gotta lay off the prosciutto, Chloe baby," Mama leaned over and told her older daughter. "It's not good for the *bambina*."

Chloe nodded, her hand still planted over her son's lips, a nervous laugh so close to the surface of her own mouth I could see her lips spasming in an attempt to keep it in.

"I'll take her." I reached down to grab the perpetual diaper bag that had become an appendage for my sister. The gratitude swimming in her eyes filled my heart.

Now that the gastronomic bomb torturing her little tummy was expelled—*Gesu*, was it ever—Arianna was all baby smiles and grins, wide awake and happy to be alive, despite her little bottom being smeared with icky baby sludge.

As silently and unobtrusively as I could—and do you know how hard it is to be unobtrusive when carrying a baby who smells like the equivalent of a sewage-treatment plant in your arms?—I made my way down the center aisle to the back of the church as Fr. Santini began the Gospel reading.

Downstairs in the basement bathroom, I managed to get Arianna changed without heaving up the extra sausage Mama had given me, although it was difficult at best. The parish ladies' room smelled like a chemical waste plant when I unwrapped the diaper and then removed it. To get to the diaper, though, I had to navigate through all Arianna's abundant layers.

Chloe had dressed her daughter as if she were going to be taking a vacation to Antarctica. In addition to the onesie over the diaper, I had to remove her little buckled shoes so I could take the baby tights off her in order to separate her legs enough to clean her baby private parts. Over the shoes and tights, Chloe had outfitted her in a fashionable baby unitard. Once I had it unsnapped and flayed backward under her back, I got the shoes off, then the tights, then the onesie, and at last, the diaper, which was now leaking watery brown liquid out the stretchy sides.

I used about fifty of the baby wipes Chloe had stored in the changing bag to get every last little bit of noxious, sticky, and gooey baby poop out of Arianna's chubby leg wrinkles and folds. Every time I wiped a spot clean, she'd wiggle and flail her legs, despite how I held her, and she wound up redirtying the wiped spot. For a brief second, I feared I wouldn't have enough towelettes to get her all cleaned and fresh.

Holding onto her, I opened the bathroom window to try and get some cool, fresh air in to circulate and rid the room of the overpowering odor.

When she was finally poop free, changed into a fresh diaper, redressed, and everything was back in the changing bag, I was sweating like a working farm animal and had to figure out a way to wash my hands since they were filled with the baby.

The sink was two yards at least from the changing table and the security strap had been removed, so I wasn't confident in letting her just lie there and hope she didn't fall off.

Now that she was wide awake, she was fidgety and squirmy.

Attempting to hold her in one hand while I washed and dried the other and then reversed the whole procedure for the other hand seemed way too hard.

Chloe had a gigantic bottle of hand sanitizer in the diaper bag she insisted everyone who held the baby slather on themselves before she'd fork her over. It was easy to squirt some on one hand and rub it into the other while my body stood guard in front of the changing table, anchoring my goddaughter in place.

All that finally done, I lifted Arianna in my arms,

doused her with sweaty, sloppy kisses, and made my way back upstairs to rejoin the mass.

Communion was just commencing. I'd missed all of Fr. Santini's first sermon.

Chloe took the baby from me and kissed me quickly on the cheek, then let me in front of her as we processed up to the altar.

I folded my hands together, prayerlike, in preparation, and to my utter horror, noticed I'd missed a large smear of baby poop on the outside fleshy part of one of my palms. If I'd been able to wash my hands properly, it wouldn't have remained.

The moment I'd noticed it visually, I also began noticing it nasally. Nonna was in front of me and I heard her take a deep, loud sniff, and then she turned her head around to me, made a pinched I-smell-something-foul face and looked down at my hands.

With eyebrows shooting almost to the back of her skull they were raised so high, she reached into her valise-sized purse and extracted a couple of tissues—*used* tissues—and shoved them into my hands.

"Use this, Gia, before the father smells you," she ordered in Italian.

Whenever Nonna doesn't want people around her who aren't family to know what she's saying, she slips into the language of her birth. My entire family was raised speaking the old language at home just so we'd be able to understand her.

Two of the tissues she'd given me were hardened and crusted together, and I didn't for the life of me want to guess what the *glue* was, so I did as I was commanded. When my turn came to receive the body of Jesus Christ, I had three crumbled up tissues tucked inside my sleeve, but my hands were poop free.

Fr. Santini lifted a wafer from the chalice and held it up in front of my face. "The body of Christ," he said in his deep, warm, and honeyed voice.

Now, even though St. Rita's is an old-fashioned parish, we do adhere to some of the newer Church dictates, such as placing the host in the parishioner's hands and allowing them to place it in their own mouths.

But.

There was no way I was going to have the Body of my Lord Jesus Christ put into hands that had the subtle aroma of baby poop and might still have some remnants of the same on them, so I tilted my chin up—way up because the good father is so tall—and silently signaled for it to be given to me in the old-school way.

A little surprise jumped in his beautiful dark eyes, but he did as requested.

I swallowed and crossed myself, marveling at the fact my pulse was staying normal, my breathing was even and low. So in contrast to yesterday.

It was clear to me my little pseudo-crush on the handsome young priest had been a fleeting one.

Grazie, Gesu. Thank you, Jesus.

I made the sign of the cross and moved on to take a sip of the sacramental wine and, *mama mia,* did I need that little nip just about then.

When mass ended, all the parishioners lined up in the back of the church to shake the new padre's hand and introduce themselves.

While we stuttered and staggered forward single file, Chloe kissed my cheek again. "You are a godsend, baby sister. Thank you."

"No worries." I tickled Arianna in her belly, and she

beamed up at me. "I don't remember Lorenzo's poop being so noxious or copious. I used almost your entire package of baby wipes."

"You gotta be careful with your foods, Chloe, like Mama told you," Daddy said from behind us, shaking his head. "I remember with Antonio, one sausage was enough to send your mama to the bathroom for an hour and give your brother belly troubles for a few days so she couldn't leave the house with him for fear of an explosion."

"I couldn't eat any cheeses with my babies. Gave me putrid gas that stank the house up for months," Aunt Gracie said in a volume not proper for church. From in front of us, some parishioners turned around and threw her annoyed stares.

When my family's turn came to overwhelm the young priest, I hung back a little, letting my parents and everyone else go first. Nonna had her usual *help me, I'm old and might fall and break a hip* death grip on my arm and wasn't letting go, even when she stuck her hand out to Fr. Santini.

She said something to him in Italian that had his eyes crinkling at the corners and a wide, pleased smile erupting across lips I'd fantasized about last night and which, bless you God, had no effect on me today.

He responded to her in Italian, charming her into a one-toothed grin of her own. I didn't want to shake his hand because I was still leery of any residual poop being transferred, so I smiled and nodded. "Thanks, Father."

He smiled back.

That was it.

No trace of recognition. No "How'd you do after I left yesterday?" Nothing to hint we'd spent the better part of an hour together, working and talking.

And in my case, lusting.

To say my ego suffered a little hit at his behavior would be true.

Oh well. I sighed as I helped Nonna into the car.

He'd probably met a hundred or more people in addition to me since yesterday. I guess I didn't leave a lasting impression. Which, in reality, was all for the better.

During the drive home, Mama told me I'd missed Fr. Santini's introduction of himself while I'd been in poop-ville with Arianna.

"He's one of ten kids." She checked her image in the car mirror again as she had when we'd driven to church. "Three brothers, six sisters. Three sets of twins. Ten pregnancies. *Madre di Dio*, that poor woman's insides."

"I had ten pregnancies," Nonna said with pride in her craggy voice. "She only had seven, 'cause the twins count as one each." Okay, pride and a little splash of maternity one-upmanship. "My doctor says I got insides that look like shredded wheat," she added, with a smug-filled smirk.

This was way too much information for me.

"So, a big family?" I said to the back of Mama's head, hoping she'd take the hint and keep talking so we'd all be spared Nonna's pregnancy horror tales.

"Yeah. One brother's in construction, and one manages a restaurant downtown. He's got a sister who's a nun, too. They're a very holy family."

"I wanted to be a nun," Nonna declared.

"You did not." Mama turned her head to face her mother.

"*Si,* Francesca. *E la verita*. It's true. I wanted to join the Little Order of the Flower. I loved the order, and the nuns were very popular in my province. So holy, so pure. All the boys back in the village were wild for me, though, and my papa needed money for the farm, so since I was the oldest girl, he married me off to your papa for two cows and a herd of goats."

"Guess who got the better part of *that* deal," Daddy said under his breath, forgetting the stealth-hearing Nonna possesses. From the backseat, and without any regard to the fact he was driving and could crash and kill us all, she clapped him on the back of his head so hard her palm turned beet red from the force.

"Hey!" Daddy rubbed his hand along his skull.

"It's your own fault," Mama said without a drop of sympathy and then reapplied her lipstick.

"She hits me again she's going in the room next to Uncle Vito at the home."

Nonna's eyes narrowed to slitty little lines, and I know she was planning some kind of silent revenge on Daddy.

Nonna never wasted a *malocchio.*

How to be a Good Italian, Lesson Four:
Keep your mouth shut
and your opinions to yourself.

Welcome to my family.

Chapter Four

Die-hard Italians do two things and two things only on Sundays. Attending mass with family is one. The other is something referred to as *il pranzo della domenica,* or the Sunday Lunch.

Most people eat their main meal in the evening on Sundays, just as they do during the workweek.

Not so, Italians. We eat our big meal—and by big, I mean humongous—in the early afternoon, usually starting between noon and one o'clock.

After mass everyone will go home to freshen up and then meet back at a chosen relative's house for the actual meal. Since Nonna is the oldest surviving parent in our immediate family and she lives in my parents' home, the relatives flock to our table every Sunday afternoon.

And so it was after Fr. Santini's first mass that my entire family was seated at Nonna's imported dining-room table again as we'd all been the night before.

Mama began cooking the moment we arrived home. Nonna had hobbled to her bedroom off the kitchen first, removed her black "church" dress, hung it back up in the closet to be worn again next Sunday, and replaced it with an identical one, straight down to the twenty buttons that lined it from shoulders to calves. For as long as my memory could recall, she'd worn no color other than black on her body.

When I'd been younger, I'd asked Nonna why all her dresses were the exact same color and style. She'd clipped me once on the side of the head and told me I had no business asking such a question. It was from Chloe I learned wearing black is a sign of reverence in our culture and that Nonna wore it out of respect and remembrance for all the deaths she'd suffered in her life: her parents, her siblings, some of her children, her beloved husband.

I could understand that, I truly could. But you'd think she'd vary the style a little. In her closet she had seven identical black dresses, one for every day of the week; three pairs of identical black orthopedic shoes; two black coats; two black spring jackets, and an assortment of sweaters in—you guessed it—black. All her undergarments were midnight colored as well.

By all accounts, my *nonna* was the most *respectful* woman to ever walk the earth.

Lunch was, as usual, loud, raucous, lit with laughter, and filling. By the time the *caffè* was served hours later, and along with it the pastries Chloe had brought, my pants were tight around my waist and I knew I couldn't eat another morsel. As my father, uncles, and brothers undid their belt buckles and popped open the top buttons on their trousers so they could consume dessert in comfort, I had an overwhelming desire to run away for a little while.

I love my family. Truly. There is no doubt of that. But sometimes all that love and togetherness can be overpowering and stifling.

"Mama, I'm gonna take a walk," I told her when I found her in the kitchen pouring a shot of *limoncello* into Nonna's *caffè*.

"You okay, *bambina?*" She cupped my chin in her strong hand and peered at me with love and concern in those all-knowing Mediterranean-blue eyes of hers.

I bent and kissed her soft cheek. Managing a smile, I said, "I'm fine. I just need a little air to clear my head."

"You got a lot going on in that smart brain of yours, with your exams and all, Gia baby. I know." She patted my cheek. "Go. *Tu vai.*"

I grabbed my coat, stuffed my laptop into my purse, and snuck out the kitchen door, not wanting anyone to join me.

Mama called after me. "If you walk by Pontevecchio's, bring me back some *pizzelles.*"

I promised her I would.

I swear on a stack of Bibles, Mama is either a mind reader or a psychic. Pontevecchio's, our neighborhood bakery, was actually where I was heading. At this time of day, I knew the shop would be quiet since most of the locals would have stopped by earlier to purchase their Sunday baked goods and desserts. I wanted that quiet, peaceful atmosphere to do a little last-minute studying and knew I could find solitude there.

The minute I opened the bakery door, my mouth started to water. The aroma of warm sugar, the doughy tang of bread yeast, and a hot blast of cinnamon all assaulted my senses. My stomach cramped with craving, forgetting it had been eating for the past four hours.

"Gia! *Come stai?*" Papa Pontevecchio called from behind the counter, his wide, toothless smile filling the bottom half of his face.

Giancarlo "Papa" Pontevecchio was of Nonna's generation and had owned the bakery for over sixty years. He should have retired thirty years ago but argued to one and all that a life spent lounging around wasn't a productive one because he had flour in his veins. So at somewhere in his nineties, he still worked six days a week, rising when other people were heading to bed, and baking the night away.

"*Ciao*, Papa. I'm fine. What are you doing here so late?" I leaned over the counter and kissed each of his wrinkled, weathered cheeks.

"Sonya went into labor this morning, and Carlo and the family's with her at the hospital."

Carlo was his great-grandson and the afternoon bakery manager; Sonya, his wife.

"*Complementi*! Congratulations."

"*Grazie*. This makes my first great-great-grandchild."

"I'll be sure to tell Nonna. She's gonna be so jealous."

He laughed, knowing my grandmother's sense of one-upmanship in everything in life.

"So, what can I get you, *bella ragazza*?"

I placed an order for Mama's *pizzelles* and ordered a small cup of espresso for myself.

"I need about a half hour on the cookies," Papa told me.

"No worries. I want to sit and chill, if you don't mind."

"Not at all."

The bakery was empty, so I grabbed a table in the corner and booted up my laptop. To say I was a little nervous about my first exam in the morning would be an understatement. Even though I was math proficient and a quick study, there were so many laws and theorems with the profession of accounting that I needed to know each and every one inside and out just in case an obscure question came up on the test.

Soon, I was engrossed in debt management, deaf and blind to everything around me. I don't know how long I sat there, sipping my delicious coffee and reading, but suddenly I heard my name.

When I looked up from my screen, a pair of gorgeous dark eyes stared down at me.

"I thought that was you."

Santini.

Looking, well, *handsome* doesn't seem strong enough a word to use, but that's what he did look like. All six foot plus of him, garbed from head to toe in inky raven black.

His wheat-colored hair was a little windblown on the top, and the tips of his ears were an adorable pink, probably from the chilly bite in the late afternoon air. He wore a black, extremely well-fitted suit jacket over his clothes that just couldn't be clerical issued. It fit as if it had been hand tailored to his perfect shoulders, and not institutionally manufactured.

Once again, that fallen angel impression drifted into my mind.

"What are you doing here?" I swear, sometimes I want to slap my own head, just like Mama and Nonna do when someone misbehaves. "I'm sorry," I told him, wincing. "That came out a little more than rude."

He laughed and pulled out the chair across from mine. "No worries. You seemed pretty engrossed in what you were reading, so I'm sorry I startled you."

Now here's the funny thing. Yesterday when we'd met, I'd been struck dumb by his hotness. This morning at mass, not so much. But right now, seated across from him, noticing how his cut-from-glass cheeks and granite jaw were just a little wind chapped from the winter weather, I got a little squirmy in my seat, a hot bead of lust tickling my thighs and points directly north of them.

"And to answer your question—" His gaze fixated on my face, while he held up a little Pontevecchio's bakery box tied with a blue string. "I've got a few hours before I need to be back on duty, and I'm on my way to visit my *nonno*. Fr. Mario mentioned this place has the best cookies in town so I wanted to bring some with me."

Awww. Why did this guy have to be an almost-priest? Why couldn't he be a red-blooded, single, straight male looking for a mate, instead of promised to the Lord?

If I didn't have bad luck, I'd have no luck, according to Uncle Sonny.

True.

"What kind?" I asked.

"Well, my family calls them venetians"—his teeth looked, befittingly, pearly-gates white when his lips opened into a smile—"but I think most people call them rainbow cookies or—"

"Seven layers." I grinned. "Those are my all-time favorites."

"Really?" If possible, his smile got even brighter. "Mine, too. I'll have to remember that."

Okay, *what?*

Why would he need to remember my favorite cookie?

"Does your grandfather live close by?" I asked for something to say.

"About six blocks from here. He's lived with my

46

uncle since my *nonna* died a few years ago."

I cocked my head to one side. "Usually, it's the girls in the family who inherit the widowed parent."

"True." He chuckled. "At the time, my mom asked him to come and live with us, but with so many kids still home, he told her he didn't want to be an added—"

"Burden," I finished.

This time he full out laughed, and the sound heated my insides like warmed milk and fresh-from-the-oven bread.

"Exactly. My uncle Nunzio's never been married, so it seemed like the perfect solution, two bachelors sharing a house. Nonno cooks and cleans, and my uncle keeps an eye on the old guy to make sure he takes his heart pills and watches his sugar intake."

"Your mom is okay with the living arrangement?"

"Pretty much. She would have preferred to have him with her, but she's just happy her dad has someone looking out for him. A slip-and-fall and broken hip is always a heartbeat away, you know? Something to worry about at his age."

I nodded and took a sip of my espresso, gagging at how cold it had grown.

How long had I been sitting here?

"So you know what it's like, I take it? First hand?" he asked.

"Yeah. My grandmother moved in with us two days after we buried my grandfather. I don't even remember there being a discussion about it. One day she was visiting. The next, she was unpacking. That slip-and-fall worry is universal, by the way, especially by the women in my house. Nonna's gotten a little frailer the past year or so, so I've been assigned as her walker whenever we go out and she's with us."

"Let me guess." His lips quirked as he lifted his chin a little and looked at me from under his lashes. "A grip like death? A begging voice pleading, "Don't let go, *bambina*, don't let go?"

I nodded and sighed, to which he laughed again. "You're a good mimic. That sounds just like her, straight down to the craggy voice. Anyway, she's been with us since I was little, so I understand the whole extended-family-living-situation thing."

His lips twitched at the corners, and I have to admit for a hot second I had the notion to stretch over and put mine firmly against them.

"We have a lot in common, you know," he said.

"*La familiglia,* for sure. "

His grin grew. "Where are you in the food chain?"

"Last of six. I was an *oops* baby. My sister, Chloe, is the closest in age to me, and she's nine years older. Daddy and Mama thought they were done when she came."

"My sister Elizabeth Ann was an *oopsie*, too. And I'll deny this if you ever tell my siblings, but she's my favorite."

Awww. "How much younger is she than you?"

"Sixteen years. She just turned eleven."

So that made him twenty-seven. "That's a lifetime. My brother Gianni is the oldest of us, and he's forty-two, eighteen years my senior. When I was a kid, he was already married. I've got a few nieces and nephews who could pass for my siblings. That gets kinda weird at times, having a seventeen-year-old call you *zia*."

"Like I said, we've got a lot in common."

This was so nice, just sitting here, having a normal

conversation with a guy. So different from all the other recent dates I'd had with guys my aunts and uncles set me up with, no-neck musclemen with comic-book educations and old-world notions on virginal brides.

With the next breath, it dawned on me this wasn't a date. Not even remotely resembling one because, *hello,* the man sitting across from me wasn't a potential love interest, but a priest.

"I bet you were a cute kid," he said, breaking through my thoughts, his eyelids going to half-mast again as his gaze swept across my face and neck. And lower.

Whoa. Flirty, much? My new cleric was giving off a very secular vibe here.

A totally hot, available-male, secular vibe.

"So, Gia San Valentino." He leaned forward, resting his elbows on the table now, his hands clasped and close to mine, that cut-to-the-bone jacket pulling against his massive shoulders. "What are you doing here on this chilly December afternoon?"

Okay, that tickling sensation between my legs? Yeah, it turned into a full-blown, thigh-rubbing clench when he said my name. He made my name sound soft, smooth, seductive, like a hot puff of wispy smoke floating on a breeze.

I crossed my legs and then too late appreciated this was absolutely the wrong thing to do. All the blood in the lower part of my body had pooled to the most private part of me. It actually pulsed—*pulsed*—when my thighs crossed over one another.

"I-I needed to get out of the house for a little while." I tried valiantly to calm the way my breath was coming in spurts. "It's Sunday, so you know, everyone's over. Everyone. It gets a little…" I shrugged.

Santini nodded and reached out to tap the top my hand. A warm bullet of awareness fired at my nerve fibers in the spot where he'd touched.

Branded. I'd been branded was all I could think.

"Too much, yeah. I get that. I've got a big family too, and although I love them all, sometimes it's just good to be alone. To get away from all the noise and commotion."

It was my turn to nod.

"I love my siblings, dearly," he said, "but with so many of us so close in age, it gets claustrophobic at times."

I'd been thinking the same thing.

He hadn't moved his hand from the top of mine, and now his index finger was doing a slow, steady crawl across my knuckles. Almost like a—*gulp*—caress.

Gesu, Gia, what the heck?

Deep down inside my brain where the logical, analytical receptors were stored, it registered that the way he was stroking my hand wasn't exactly proper behavior or accepted touch for an almost-priest. But in the area where my emotions, feelings, and desires lived? Well, that bunch was screaming, "Hell, yeah!"

I couldn't move my hand.

Okay, let's be honest. I didn't *want* to move my hand. Ever.

The mix of confusing and conflicting emotions bowling through my system regarding this guy was beginning to get to me. One minute, just staring at him and hearing his voice could turn me to mush; the next, it was like I was talking to my brother. And now, well, my heart was pounding, and my skin was prickling and tingling like a live, spliced wire was electrifying through it at just his simple touch.

While he continued with his absentminded finger stroking, we engaged in a mutual staring competition sweltering enough to start me sweating. The deep cognac and brighter gold flecks in his eyes were mesmerizing, and I couldn't look away from them.

Mama had raised us with the notion that staring was one of the rudest things you could do, so I avoided it as much as possible. But right now, in the middle of Pontevecchios's on a chilly December Sunday afternoon, I couldn't look away from the delectable man in front of me.

I wanted to shrug out of my jacket because my armpits were dripping—as was another place on me—but that would mean I'd have to pull my hand away from the table where he was—*God help me*—fondling it. There was no way in hell I was going to do that. The moment I thought of hell, the notion I was paving my way straight there with my actions and thoughts danced a vigorous tarantella across my mind.

"You know"—his gaze wandered across my face—"I had a lot of fun yesterday at the festival setup. Much more than I thought I would. I was sorry I had to leave so soon."

Swallowing, I simply nodded. I couldn't get my brain synapses to fire to form a coherent response. Everything about him, from the way his gaze raked across my lips and back up to my own eyes to linger, to the rhythmic back and forth trailing of his index finger across my knuckles, even to the subtle yet totally intoxicating scent of clean soap and man drifting from him, floated through me.

I hadn't had a drop of real alcohol in weeks (dinner wine doesn't count), but I felt drunk just being in his presence. Drunk with desire, with need, with, *Madre di Dio*, longing.

I couldn't read what was written in his eyes, but when his tongue skimmed across his lower lip and he leaned in a little closer to me across the table, I knew without a doubt that I had to put an end to this.

Mio Dio, we were in a public place where I was as well known as the owners. If someone recognized me or if any members of my connected family walked in and found me locked in a lust-filled eye orgy with the new parish priest, a priest who was, for lack of a better term, making love to my hand, I would be sure to not only suffer the fires of the underworld for all eternity, but before suffering that fate, my life would be turned into a living, breathing hell by my parents.

Just when I decided I really needed to pull my hand away and get a grip on the reality of this situation, Papa called out my name from the counter.

"Got ya *pizzelles* ready, Gia."

I blinked. Hard. My flickering eyelids must have looked like I was tapping out Morse code, because Santini squeezed my hand. "You okay, Gia?"

This was becoming the question of the decade with people where I was concerned.

I had to physically will my hand to release itself from his. His fingers were long, straight, and solid. The nails and cuticles cared for, not in a fussy, metrosexual way, but in a man-who-was-conscious-of-his-appearance way.

I had to get away from this guy. Once you start noticing the way a man grooms his hands, you need to put some distance between the two of you because this will lead to other thoughts. Forbidden thoughts. Impure thoughts. Thoughts like what would those hands feel like trailing across your naked flesh? What would they be able to do to set your pulse endings on fire? Make you scream in ecstasy? Make you want to die for pleasure?

This man was forbidden on all counts. On every count.

"I-I need to go. To get home. They're waiting. My family is waiting. For me. For the *pizzelles*."

Gesu. Now I was babbling, and that was never a good sign.

"Gia—"

"Have a fun visit with your grandfather." I stood and threw my laptop into my bag. "I know he's gonna love the cookies. Like Fr. Mario told you, they're the best in town."

Papa stood at the counter, my *pizzelle* box wrapped and waiting. He held it up, and I grabbed it.

"I'll put it on your mama's account," he told me, his lifted-eyebrow gaze shifting from me to Santini and then back to me. "*Nessum problema*." No worries.

If he only knew.

I nodded and threw a final "See you in church," over my shoulder to Santini.

Outside, the wind had picked up and slapped me silly when I went through the door. I welcomed the frigid blast. I needed it to cool me down physically, emotionally, and, God forgive me, sexually.

Why in the name of all that's holy and good did I react in such an out-of-control way toward him? I was all set to jump across the table and into his lap at one point.

I'd never acted this way with any guy. I'd never been in such a desire-filled haze that I forgot everything I'd ever been taught about how a good girl behaves.

The one time I hadn't reacted to him like a sex-starved *puttana* was when he'd said mass that morning. Why not?

And then it hit me.

Could it really be as simple as that? Seeing him in his church vestments turned off any and all sexual thoughts about him. He was still as handsome as sin, but it hadn't affected me in the least. It was only when he was garbed in regular cleric clothes that my brain went haywire.

Maybe I should just picture him in priestly attire every time I came in contact with him in the future.

I mulled this over as I sprinted home, the *pizzelle* box secure in my arms.

Chapter Five

Monday morning broke clear, cold, and way too fast for me. I had to be in lower Manhattan by eight a.m. to take the first part of my licensing exams, and since I hadn't gone to bed until after two due to the last-minute nervous and stress-filled studying I'd tried to cram in, I was cranky, tired, and a little nauseous. Sleep had further eluded me due to constant images of a fair-haired man of the cloth drifting before my eyes.

Mama and Nonna had been up since four, Mama because of the postmenopausal insomnia that ruled her life and Nonna because she'd been a life-long farm girl, up before the first light, halfway done with chores by daybreak, and old habits died hard.

I would have been happy to be the only one awake and spared the coaxing and commanding to eat a huge breakfast to "help my brain." All I wanted was coffee to wake me up and little bit of chocolate as a de-stressor. With these two domineering, mothering woman, that wasn't about to happen.

I begged off a second helping of eggs, toast, and sausage and calculated if I avoided putting on any makeup, I would have a few extra minutes to run into a chain coffee shop and grab an extra-large cup of caffeine to go.

As I was dashing out the door, Mama stopped me and shoved a stuffed brown paper bag into my hands.

"Take this, Gia baby. It's a *piccolo spuntino* for when you have a break. You gotta keep your brain cells nourished."

The *piccolo spuntino*, or little snack, she handed me was enough to feed a family of four. It was so heavy that when I put it in my messenger bag my shoulder drooped, and I had to walk with my left hip pushed out to balance.

"Kiss the Holy Father for luck," she ordered before she'd let me out the door.

Because, *really*, I had no recourse, I did. Then because it was expected, I crossed myself. With a last quick buss to Mama's cheek and a loud "*Ciao*, Nonna," I bolted out the door and jogged the four blocks to the downtown train.

The morning session of tests went by so fast, before I realized it, lunchtime rolled around and I was actually hungry. I had an hour and a half to kill before the afternoon session started, so I left the building for some needed fresh air and sunshine.

Two weeks before Christmas is not the time to be ambling casually around lower Manhattan. The holiday shopping hordes were larger than usual due to the unexpected, but lovely, warmer weather we'd woken to, and the sidewalks were chock-full with illegal vendors and hawkers trying to interest anyone and everyone in their "bargain-priced" items. As I left the testing center, I spotted a guy trying to unload designer handbags I knew sold at retail for over five hundred bucks each, for thirty dollars. They had to have fallen off a truck, as Mama would say.

I wondered if the vendor knew my Uncle Sonny.

It took me almost five minutes to cross the street

from the testing center to Battery Park. I wanted some quiet time to myself to think, eat, and wind down a little, and sitting in the park, watching the harbor boats, was my idea of self-soothing.

I found a quiet bench in front of the seawall, planted myself on it, and took Mama's brown bag from my purse. As I'd predicted, her small snack was anything but.

She'd sent me out with a liter bottle of Pellegrino, a full-sized sub sandwich on her homemade ciabatta bread, cut into two six-inch portions laden with prosciutto, provolone, a healthy splash of olive oil, sliced garden tomatoes, a few peppers, and some romaine lettuce. In a separate plastic container, she'd added two cannoli and three biscotti.

Francesca San Valentino, the patron saint of carbs.

It was a wonder we all didn't weight five hundred pounds eating like this every day.

I settled into my seat and dug in.

The harbor water was calm, an effect of the warm weather, but listening to it slap and splash in a gentle staccato against the tugboat planks filled me with a relaxing and centering peace. I hadn't had a moment to think about my life and my future for some time. I'd been studying like crazy for the licensing exams, and living at home was never a quiet place to be, with my various family members drifting in and out every day.

And let's be honest: we weren't exactly what you'd call a quiet bunch.

At twenty-four, I still lived under my parents' roof, had no full-time paying job other than occasionally helping my father with his business books and those of a few of his business associates, and my love life was nonexistent.

It wasn't that I didn't get asked out. I did. Often. Plus, I was perpetually being set up by the aunts and uncles. I'd had a steady boyfriend all through high school, but we went our separate ways when we graduated. My choices had been limited in recent years to guys I met in college—who were all looking to score, not forge a life-time commitment—and then in accounting school who were, for lack of a better word, boring and absorbed either in numbers theory, finding jobs after graduation, or in just getting into my pants. The men my extended family routinely set me up with were mostly rough around the edges, wise-guy wannabes who wanted a conventional Italian bride they could keep barefoot, pregnant, and cooking.

So. Not. Me.

I needed to make some decisions about my life, and make them soon. First, pass the exams and get licensed. That accomplished, I could then look for a real job so I could afford to live on my own. This one might be the hardest to bring about since my parents were old-school thinkers who believed girls should stay home until they were married. They couldn't understand why I didn't want to go from their house to a husband's house, and never experience what it would be like living on my own.

Lastly, I wanted to find the one special guy I could commit to. A guy who'd be family oriented like me, want kids, the minivan, a house in the 'burbs, the whole family-comes-first-and-always mentality I'd been breastfed on.

I wasn't too picky. Obviously, I didn't want him to look like a troll, but nice looking wouldn't hurt since I'd be spending eternity staring across the kitchen table at his face. A job that paid well would be nice in a career where I didn't need to worry he'd make one wrong move and wind up as fish food in the Meadowlands marshes.

Don't laugh. Have I mentioned my Uncle Sonny?

A flash of mink-colored eyes passed in front of my mind, and my pulse kicked up a little at the memory of how they'd been focused on me at the volunteer setup and then again yesterday in the bakery. He'd been so intent on studying me, listening to me tell him about my family, sharing his own thoughts. If he hadn't been a man of God, I swear, he'd have been the best first date I'd ever had.

But our meeting hadn't been a first date, and he *was* a man of God.

In the next breath, I heard my name in a voice that warmed my entire body like a shot of fine, aged brandy.

I looked up, and the pair of eyes I'd been daydreaming about just a moment ago was staring straight at me, grinning from etched cheekbone to etched cheekbone.

"It's my turn to ask this," he said, as he sat down next to me. "What are you doing here?"

Words wouldn't form in my brain. I could only stare at him, mute.

He looked, well— *Amazing* is the only word I can come up with. He'd been handsome as sin dressed all in black. Even his godly vestments hadn't been able to dull his attractiveness. But today he was in purely civilian clothes, and my toes curled in my boots when I got a look at the total package.

A light blue chambray button-down shirt under

another down vest, this one dark blue, covered his lengthy torso. Today he wore jeans—or I should say they wore him. Faded, split at one knee, they hugged his trim waist and thick thighs as snugly as when my nephew Lorenzo throws his chubby arms around me and squeezes a hug in his full-body contact, two-year-old way. Work boots, the color washed out and worn and earning their name, finished him off.

I'd never seen any man connected to the church *not* garbed in the standard-issue black from head to toe. It's weird, but I don't think I'd ever even imagined Fr. Mario in anything other than his clerical clothes, collar included.

Santini continued to gaze at me, killer smile in place, waiting for my reply.

Earth to Gia: *Wake up!*

"I…I have exams today…licensing exams."

"Oh, yeah? What for?"

"CPA. Accounting." Why I needed to clarify the initials I have no idea.

"No kidding? My cousin Rocco's a CPA," Santini said. "He works uptown at some big financial firm. Gabriel Mooney. Ever heard of it?"

I nodded. Who hadn't? Gabriel Mooney was one of the most desired accounting firms in the city to be associated with. I'd have given them Mama's secret coffee-cake recipe as a bribe just to be considered for an interview.

"Accounting's a hard field. You must be a math whiz."

I shrugged. "Some people are good at writing, some at science. I like math. Numbers come easy to me."

"Those tests are killers, though. I remember Rocco

didn't sleep for two weeks before he took them. And I think he failed the first time."

"I won't fail," I declared with a little more determination than I actually felt.

He grinned, winked an eye against the sunlight at me, and my toes erupted into little tingly spasms, every podiatric nerve fiber firing.

"Good attitude. So you're on lunch break?" he asked, glancing down at my lap where Mama's half-eaten sandwich sat.

"Yes." Finally, something synapsed in my brain allowing me to speak articulately again, so I asked him, "Would you like some? Mama must have thought I was going to be gone for a few days. She made enough to last."

He laughed and cocked his head, and I swear I lost all the feeling from my knees downward.

"You don't mind?"

"Please." I swatted my hand in the air. "You'll do me a favor if you eat some of it, because I can't possibly finish it all. If I bring it back home, I'll get asked if I'm sick, and if I throw it away, well, that's more sin than I want to commit today."

The word sin made me remember what he was. I could feel my neck start to flush with embarrassment.

Santini just grinned and ignored the comment. I handed him the half of ciabatta sandwich I had left, and he said, "Thanks. I didn't have time for breakfast before I left this morning."

"You're not on duty today?" I asked, still confused about why he wasn't in his clerical outerwear. I just assumed priests wore them all the time, whether they were at the church, or not.

"On duty? No." He cocked his head. "Not until later. I'm helping a buddy move into his new office this morning. I had to run to the bank on business and was planning on grabbing something from a street cart for lunch when I spotted you." He took a huge bite of the sandwich, and I suddenly wished I was a pepper on its way to his mouth.

Gesu, Gia.

"This is way better," he said, after swallowing. "Thanks."

I nodded, words failing me again.

Yesterday morning I'd been convinced my strange, erotic feelings for him had been a passing fancy. I'd been able to sit before him in church and then smile at him afterward without any kind of awareness of him as a hunky, gorgeous male filtering through me. Now, seated next to him on this park bench, just like I'd been in the bakery, all I could do was wish I was in his lap, his tongue swiping across my mouth like it was doing to his own at the moment.

Maybe I was right: in his cassock he looked like a priest, so I could remember he was one, and my unconscious thoughts wouldn't see him as a normal male. When he wore his regular clothes, I was able to forget his profession and in turn lust after him without guilt attached.

"I never asked you yesterday, but did you get all the Christmas lights strung for the festival?" he asked.

I nodded. "It took about another three hours, but yes. After they were all in place, we plugged them in and thankfully, they all worked."

I'd added the last part because Mama had gotten the lights from one of Uncle Sonny's *friends*, and when

Sonny is involved, you just never know how things are going to turn out.

"Sorry I had to bail on you."

"No worries," I said. "It all got done."

"The festival starts tomorrow, right?"

I nodded and took a sip of my Pellegrino. "Opening is at nine in the morning, and closing time is nine at night. I've got second shift for our family booth."

"What are you selling?"

He'd finished the sandwich, practically inhaling it, so I offered the container with the desserts.

"You're sure?" he asked.

"Please. My hips can only stand storing so much food in them in a day, and I still have to eat dinner with my parents tonight."

His mouth took its time slanting from one corner of his cheeks to the other. Really, he should have come with some kind of warning label: *Gaze upon at your own risk. Smile can be addicting.*

Through half-closed eyes, he raked a glance down to my lap, then back up to my face. "Your hips look pretty perfect from where I'm sitting," right before he pulled one of Mama's cannoli out of the container.

Whoa. Definitely getting the flirting vibe again, and this time there was no doubt it really was a flirty remark. In no way was this appropriate. No man of the cloth should say things like this, especially to a female parishioner.

But then, why didn't it feel wrong? Deep down? Why did it feel and sound so…right?

He took a bite of the cannoli, and I was struck dumb when a dusting of powdered sugar stuck to his top lip.

Can I tell you just how much I wanted to lean over

and lick every last morsel and sprinkle of it off him?

Just as I was thinking this, his tongue skimmed over his lips, and every trace of the sugar went with it.

Boy, was I jealous of that sugar.

A soft moan blew from him while he swallowed the rest of the dessert in two bites.

"That was insane," he said, wiping his lips with the back of his hand.

"I know," I said with a sigh and a grin. "Mama's cannoli are to die for."

"I would marry you in a heartbeat just to eat like this every day."

He laughed out loud and cocked his head at me again, and I swear on the Holy Father's rosary beads my insides stopped working.

Inappropriate, much? Yeah. But you know, at the moment I just didn't care.

"So, what are you selling at the festival?" he asked again.

I swallowed the dry, nervous ball of confusion lodged in my throat.

"Mama and Nonna make sauce from our garden tomatoes every year. We grow so many during the summer there's no way we can ever eat them all, and the sauce is Nonna's family recipe. Mama cans over two hundred quarts a year"—he whistled at the number— "plus what we save for ourselves, and she sells the rest, donating most of the money to the parish for the St. Vincent De Paul coffers."

"If the sauce tastes as good as what you just shared with me, I'll make sure I buy a couple jars for my mother. Especially since the proceeds go to such a worthy cause."

"Oh, you don't have to. Mama always gives a case to Fr. Mario for the rectory's use every year. I actually think she does it to keep on his good side and in his good graces."

I bit down on my tongue, horrified when I realized I'd essentially just told him we bribed his boss so he'd be nice to us.

His brows beetled above his gorgeous eyes, but he was stopped from saying something when one of the harbor tugboat horns blared from a spot in the water close to us.

It sounded like a cannon booming but served to divert whatever he was going to say.

Nervous doesn't begin to describe how I felt. Why could I not keep my stupid thoughts in my head, or my mouth shut, around this man? It was like my brain turned off my inhibition center whenever I spoke to him.

With a quick jerk, I shoved the remnants of lunch back into the paper bag and stood.

He did as well.

The feeling of being dwarfed in his presence overtook me again, since I needed to bend my head way back to see his face.

"I've gotta get back to the exam center," I said. "The afternoon session starts in a few minutes."

"Gia—" He reached out and slid a hand around my upper arm, stopping me.

I think I gasped. I know, like Lot's wife, I turned into a pillar of petrified salt and stood stone still, all freedom of movement driven from me.

He took a step closer, peering down at my face, into my eyes, into my very soul.

"I—"

"Look—" he said at the same time.

We both clammed up.

His back was to the midday sun, its brightness haloing his head, allowing those little specks of gold and amber to sparkle freely in his eyes, pressing against the darker outer circle. I couldn't quite read the expression written in them, but they were moist and so filled with warmth all I wanted to do was stare at them—and him—for the rest of the day.

Who am I kidding? I wanted to stare at him for the rest of my life.

Just like in the church parking lot, all the normal midday noise and commotion surrounding us faded. I couldn't hear the soothing slap of the water against the dock any longer; couldn't hear the voices of the people walking around us in the park; couldn't see anything but this beautiful man standing in front of me, holding my arm, and my total attention, in his hands.

His lips parted, and his tongue swirled across his bottom lip.

Sweet Mother of God, I wanted to tug it into my mouth with such a longing it made my insides jiggle like overcooked linguini.

Just as the idea came and settled, his head inched down to mine. All sense of propriety flew as I matched his movement, rising up higher on my toes to meet him.

Neither one of us closed our eyes, as if doing so would somehow spoil the moment. I was hypnotized by the circles of light and dark in his irises. He didn't even blink. Not once.

The last coherent thought I had before his lips touched mine was *what in the name of all that's holy are you doing, Gia?*

A sensation of almost unbearable heat surged through me when our lips came together.

Patiently, just touching and nothing more, we kissed. From somewhere far off, my sense of hearing returned and the deepest, softest, most wistful sigh I'd ever heard sailed into me expelled straight from somewhere deep inside him.

His lips pressed more firmly, possessively, fully, against mine.

From the inner recesses of my nonfunctioning brain, it occurred to me that this, *this,* is what a kiss should feel like. Sweet, but arousing. Complete, but leaving you wanting more.

Never had a simple kiss made me ache.

Before I could stop them, my hands dropped the forgotten lunch bag and floated up his torso, over the soft, pliant feel of his vest, to wind around his neck and cross behind it. My fingertips skimmed the collar on his soft-as-velvet shirt and then threaded upward until I could twine them in his close-cropped hair. I was on the very tips of my booted toes unable to move up any further unless I jumped and wrapped my legs around his waist, which believe me, I considered, when he bent further to meet me halfway.

He pulled me in so close there wasn't a whisper of room between our bodies, save for our clothing. So close I could feel his heart hammering against me, his chest rising and falling with every breath as fast as pumping accordion bellows. So close, in fact, there was no masking the unmistakable feel of his arousal pulsing against my belly.

Madre di Dio.

My lips opened on a lust-filled cry, and his tongue

wasted no time slipping in and joining with mine.

His mouth may have felt like a warm blanket, wrapping and snuggling me in its heat, but the touch of his tongue against mine was like boiling volcanic lava spreading though my system, lighting me on fire and burning a path straight to my soul.

With a subtle move, he changed the angle of the kiss so he could delve in deeper, and pressed his massive hands across my butt, pushing me even nearer until I was all but wearing him.

Every little tug and nip of my tongue with his dropped another bead of red-hot longing down to my girlie parts, which were now wet, throbbing, and—*blessed Lord, forgive me*—seeking release.

It was a good thing he was holding me or else, like a melting Italian lemon-ice on a hot summer day, I would have been a puddle of colored water on the ground beneath us.

His fingers slipped into the back pockets of my jeans, curling under the curve of my backside, almost lifting me off my toes.

My hands clamped around his neck even tighter, a tiny, scared but wickedly excited gasp shooting up from my lungs.

His heart beat a wild *tarantella* against his vest. I could feel it pounding against mine, my own keeping in perfect time to his, a dancing partner I could see spending a lifetime with.

No other man's kiss had ever done this to me, stripped me of any and all free will, made me feel as if we were the only two people on earth.

He shunted his knee along my own, insinuating his leg into the top of my thighs, separating them, and sliding along the hottest part of me.

I knew, *knew,* he had to feel how damp I was, how much my body wanted him, was prepared for him.

Heaven above, this was insane.

I was standing out in the open practically having sex with my clothes on with a man who was pledged to another. And not just any other, but *God Almighty* himself.

This was not the same Gia San Valentino who left her parents' comfortable brownstone this morning, secure in the knowledge that she was a good and obedient God-fearing Italian girl. No, this Gia was someone I didn't recognize: a wanton risk taker with absolutely no control of her body or mind.

And you know what? In the moment, I didn't even care.

Pressed up against him, his warm breath skimming over my cheeks as he kissed his way down to my jaw, then back up to my lips again, I didn't think about anything but how wonderful, how perfect, how right it was to be in his arms.

There are some things in life you know without ever knowing *why* you know them. You'll always love your family no matter what happens; you'll love your children no matter what stupid messes they get into; you'll always have your faith.

These things are givens. You know them before you realize you know them.

Standing in Battery Park, my lips pressed against Tim Santini's, I knew without a doubt no one would ever kiss me like this again no matter how long I lived.

I truly can't tell you how long we stood there wrapped in one another's arms, but it felt like forever and yet not nearly long enough.

The tugboat horn split the air again, causing enough of a blast to jolt us apart when we heard it.

We were both breathing as if we'd just climbed Mt. Etna barefoot on a sweltering August day and were in need of air and cold water.

I don't know what he saw on my face, but on his was complete, utter bafflement and total confusion, mixed with undisguised, blatant, and full arousal.

I knew just how he felt.

His lips were kiss-slicked wet and swollen, his beautiful eyes dilated to where all I could see was the inky black of his pupils. A tiny pulse bounded in his neck, and for a hot second, I wanted to rub my lips across it and suck hard.

My hands slowly came down from his neck to the spot he'd just kissed, and I dragged one finger across my mouth, a mouth which now ached and throbbed.

"Gia," he said. "Gia, I'm sor—"

I didn't let him finish. I couldn't.

Supreme humiliation and shame warred with longing.

The mortification won.

I shoved my hand up over his mouth, silencing him. His free hand wound around my wrist, encircled it, and then he traced a kiss across my palm, keeping my hand prisoner in his.

I snatched it back as if it had been scorched in hellfire.

"Don't," I whispered. Shock consumed me like a lit matchstick on dry grass. I couldn't wrench my eyes from his face. "I can't do this. *We* can't do this." I threw my messenger bag over my shoulder and across my chest. "I've got to go. I've got to get away from you."

"Gia, please. Let me explain—"

"No. No." My head was spinning, and I couldn't get away from him fast enough. "No explanations can make this right. We're going to burn in hell for eternity."

"No, we're not. Gia, please—"

I shook my head so violently spots formed in front of my eyes. "You're—I'm—I can't." Tears of frustration and yearning swelled in my eyes, and when I blinked, they began cascading down my cheeks. "It's forbidden," I said through a sob. "*You're* forbidden."

His mouth dropped open, and through my disgrace, I watched his head shake, his brows kiss in the middle over eyes that narrowed to slits.

"What?" He reached out to take my hand, but I slapped it away. "Please, Gia, listen to me—"

"I've got to go. I've got to. Go. Please." Heedless of the garbage I'd dropped on the ground, and without another word, I sprinted away from him as fast as I could, holding onto my messenger bag with both hands as if my life depended on it.

Just like the night before when I'd run from the bakery, I never looked back. Running faster than I think I've ever moved before, I darted across the traffic, heedless of the moving cars all around me, and back to the exam center.

What had I just done? What in the name of all that was holy had just happened? Had I lost my mind? My reason? I couldn't begin to count the number of sins I'd just committed.

And more importantly than anything else, what was I going to do about it now?

Chapter Six

Walking home from the train three hours later, I was still reeling.

I'd been kissed by a priest.

A priest.

Well, okay, for the purposes of full disclosure, an almost-priest since he hadn't been ordained yet. But regardless. He was a man who had no business kissing a woman, any woman.

And it wasn't a simple, chaste, little buss of his lips on my cheek. The kind you'd give a child or an elderly relation.

No.

It had been a full-out, tongue-mating, inside-quaking, panty-dropping kiss filled with passion, longing, and—again, blessed Lord, forgive me—absolute and total lust.

On both our parts, because not only had *he* kissed me, *I'd* kissed him back.

Boy, had I. No thoughts of what I was doing or with whom had stopped me. In all honesty, I don't think anything short of being forcibly wrenched away from him by someone else would have stopped me from responding to his kiss.

Which, I kept asking myself, was worse? His initiation of the kiss or my response to it?

We were both culpable for our actions, so I couldn't

find a satisfying answer to the question.

I don't have any memory of finishing up the exam. I could have failed and gone down in accounting flames, or sailed through it with a perfect score, for all I knew.

Somehow I made it back home after the testing finished for the day and—thank you, Jesus—the house was empty. Daddy, I knew, was at work, and since this was Monday, Mama and Nonna were at the nursing home visiting Uncle Vito, Nonna's older brother.

I had the house to myself for at least another hour. There was no way I would have held up to Mama's scrutiny or Nonna's sixth sense had they been home when I arrived. They would have descended on me like hungry lions on prey—mercilessly—sucking my bones dry of any and all information, because they would have known something out of the ordinary had happened to me. Something monumental and soul changing. Something I didn't want to share. With anyone. Ever.

I should have felt unclean, dirty, hellbound.

Why I didn't was unsettling, to say the least.

When Tim Santini's mouth had claimed mine, I'd responded like I'd never done before to any other kiss. I'd quite simply lost my mind of all sensible function when our lips met and mated.

Of course, I'd been kissed before. Even an overprotected twenty-four-year-old Italian girl and baby of the family who still lived at home with her parents, had found occasions to be kissed.

I'd been kissed well, and not so well.

I'd been kissed by teenaged boys who were nervous, unsure, and sloppy.

I'd been kissed by grown men who were experienced, cocky, and rehearsed.

But never—never—had I been kissed like Tim kissed me. In his arms I'd felt wanted, cherished, desired. The sense that I knew the taste of him as well as I knew the taste of Mama's cooking was overwhelming.

Our mouths and our bodies seemed to be forged for one another, two halves making a whole. Like red sauce and pasta. Cannoli shells and ricotta cheese.

It was a good thing we were out in the open with scores of people shuffling past us, because if we'd been alone, I can't really say with any certainty we wouldn't have been buck naked and having mind-blowing sex.

Being held by him was perfection, felt meant to be, mysterious and familiar all at the same time.

But it couldn't be familiar. I hadn't known he existed until two days ago. And much more importantly, we were banned from being together.

Unlike Eve, I knew what awaited me if I succumbed to my desires. I knew what to expect by giving into the temptation of the proverbial apple, and I didn't want to wind up in hell for all eternity.

So however much Tim Santini's kiss seemed right to me, it was wrong in an incalculable number of ways, and there was only one way a good little Italian girl who'd sinned could right a wrong.

I needed to confess.

It was the only way I knew my conscience could be absolved.

****

The trek twenty blocks away and across town from my house to a church not my own was slow moving due to the holiday crunch of people out on the streets and the rush-hour time frame. But I had to make it. There was no way I could go to St. Rita's and confess. Fr. Mario knew my voice since he'd known me from birth. The man had baptized me, for goodness' sake. Other than my family, he was the most recognizable, most consistent person in my life.

And what could I say to him?

"Bless me, Father, for I have sinned. It's been one week since my last confession, and today I played tonsil hockey with the guy who was sent to replace you."

Yeah, like that was ever gonna happen.

No, my only option was to go to another church where I wasn't known.

The interior of the Church of the Immaculate Conception was almost identical to St. Rita's since it hailed from the same era. The difference was in the size and scope. St. Rita's is more of a neighborhood parish, where Immaculate Conception is more of a borough church and as such, is three times the size. Like St. Rita's, the church was decked out for Christmas.

Confession was listed on the church's announcement board as every day from 8-8:30 a.m., 4-5:30 p.m., and Saturdays from 2-4 p.m.

It was almost five thirty now, and I was behind one elderly woman sitting in the waiting pew, knitting. Three parishioners had gone into the confessional booth so far, and with any luck, I would be the last one in and then be on my way back home in time to sit down to dinner.

Absolved.

Even though I didn't know anyone associated with this parish, I'd donned a sort of disguise before I left the house. I'd taken one of Nonna's endless supply of black widow's shawls and draped it over my head, covering my hair and wrapping it snugly around my neck. How she wore these things mystified me. The material was coarse and stiff and unbearably hot. I was sweating just sitting and waiting in the pew. I'd put on an old, knee-length coat I found in the back of the hall closet. I couldn't remember who it belonged to, but it didn't matter, because it offered me a cloak of unrecognizability.

The confessional opened, and an elderly, wizened, tiny bald man shuffled out. He was wearing an old horsehair coat, fashionable when Nonna was a young bride, and held a fedora with a cut-to-size peacock feather stuck in the brim, in his hands.

The knitter stood when he came out and met up with him at the end of the pew. With her arm linked through his, they tottered down the center aisle and to the back of church, each leaning on the other for support.

My little Italian-girl romantic heart sighed as I went into the now-empty confessional booth.

The privacy screen slid open, and the priest said, "Good evening."

There was something slightly recognizable in the deep, hushed voice, but I couldn't place it.

"Good evening, Father."

A beat of heavy silence echoed in the small cubicle.

"Do you have something to confess, my child?"

"Uh, yes, Father, I do."

"Go ahead, please."

Again, a little note of familiarity shot through me.

"Bless me, Father, for I have sinned. It's been a week since my last confession."

I stopped. While I knew I had to confess what I'd done, I couldn't for the life of me figure out how to say it delicately. I hadn't gotten this far in my thinking while I'd been waiting. How do you confess carnal thoughts and actions about a priest to a brother priest?

"Um," I said, trying to stall for time. "I, uh, took the Lord's name in vain twice in anger. I had disrespectful thoughts about my grandmother."

I stopped and chewed on my bottom lip.

"Go on, Gia," the voice said. "I'm listening."

Holy macaroni.

"Father Mario?" I screeched, finally putting a person to the voice.

"Lower your voice, child," he said in the same modulated, nap-inducing tone he uses at mass.

"What are you doing here?" I whisper-shrieked, my stomach muscles shaking like a pair of maracas.

"Fr. Duncan is out with a broken leg. I'm assisting his parish for a few weeks."

"Oh." So much for my attempt at remaining incognito.

Gesu.

"Child, why are you here at confession instead of St. Rita's?" he asked in the next breath, suspicion dripping from his subdued voice.

I was saved by God's intervention: my cell phone blasted an instrumental version of "Mama Said." Guess whose ring tone?

"Oops, forgive me, Father. I've got to take this."

I bolted from the confessional with the sound of Fr. Mario's voice chastising me at my back and straight into the arms of a fully cassocked Fr. Santini.

Could this day get any worse?

Braced between his outstretched hands, I gaped at him, utterly astounded and feeling like the universe was plotting against me for some heinous wrong I'd committed against humanity.

His hands were firm, and his grip strong around my arms, but I was filled with indignation and pent-up humiliation, so when I shoved them off me with my free hand, he let them fall to his sides.

He stood, rooted, in front of me, a quizzical squint in his gorgeous eyes, his full lips pointing downward at the corners.

"Are you okay?" he asked. His voice was quiet and low, his tone reverential since he was in the house of the Lord.

My phone knew no such veneration for the location and continued its loud blaring ring, now echoing up to the rafters in the empty church. I hit the play icon and then whispered, "Hold on, Mama." My gaze never broke from his.

Santini waited, his hands folded in front of him, shoulders relaxed, an air of quiet internal reflection so in contrast to the tsunami of emotions rolling through me that I wanted to hit him.

Hard.

I didn't, though. Couldn't.

He repeated his question, while Mama's voice cackled from the speaker.

"Gia? Gia? What's going on?"

I nodded to the man I'd almost had public sex with only hours before, and without another look at him, bolted out the back door of the church.

Once out on Seventh Avenue, I took a huge breath and said into my phone, "Sorry. I couldn't talk."

"Gia baby, where are you?" Mama asked, her voice filled with tears.

Chloe was a master deflector growing up and had taught me some very worthwhile tricks for dealing with our parents when they asked questions we didn't want to answer. I used one of them now.

"Why? Where are you? What's wrong?" I asked, not answering her question.

"Oh, baby, I'm at the home. Uncle Vito"—sob, sob—"he's not too long for this world."

She sniffled again, and Nonna's voice echoed in the background. "*Fermati*, Francesca. Stop crying."

"*Mama*." Even though Uncle Vito was basically brain-fried from lack of oxygen during his heart attack and had an annoying habit of flashing his naked and shriveled old-man private parts at everyone who came into his room, he was still family.

"I'll be there as soon as I can." I put my hand up to hail a cab. "I'm getting a taxi right now."

"Okay, baby," she said with a huge sob following. "Can you call Chloe?" *Sniff, sniff.*

I told her I would.

Twenty minutes later, the cab dropped me off at St. Michael the Archangel Long-Term Nursing Facility for the Sick and Dying, or as my family simply called it, *the home.*

I signed the visitor book in the lobby, nodded at the fully habited nun who served as the front-desk guard dog, and took the elevator to the third floor where Uncle Vito had spent the last five of his ninety-six years, after he'd succumbed to a massive coronary at the race track, where, paradoxically, he'd been the trifecta winner of the day.

The one hundred and forty-seven thousand dollars he'd won had paid for one night's stay in the coronary care unit after he was admitted.

Medicare took care of the rest.

Even if I hadn't known which room was my great-uncle's, I would have found it the moment I exited the elevator. The sound of wailing and keening instinctively drew me like a moth to a lit candle. There was literally a throng of people, young and old, standing outside his room. Some were crying openly, others whimpering. Most had their heads bowed, whether in prayer or something else, and all clasped rosary beads in their hands. I spotted Mama in the center of the crowd, and she shoved her way over to me.

"Gia baby." She wound her arms around my waist and planted her head on my shoulder. "It's almost time."

"Mama, what happened? I thought Uncle Vito was stable."

"The doctor thinks he had a stroke. A big one. He's not gonna come out of this, baby." She dabbed at her dripping nose with an Italian lace handkerchief I recognized as Nonna's.

I patted her back, feeling useless, as she sobbed against me. I held her and glanced around, realizing how long it had been since I'd visited my great-uncle. The last time I was in this building, the staff had decorated the walls with autumn leaves and paper pumpkins. Today, cut-out snowflakes and cardboard jingle bells filled the walls.

Mama, who'd had her hands clasped around my waist, suddenly pulled back, her gaze drifting over my torso.

"Why are you wearing my old coat?" She lifted her gaze to where I'd wrapped Nonna's headscarf around my neck. With her index finger and thumb, she pinched the material and rubbed it. "And this is Nonna's. Why do you have it?"

This was penance for trying to disguise myself. I hadn't even thought about what I was wearing when I'd hailed the cab to get to the home.

"Gia?" Mama's pencil-thin eyebrows pulled into a flat line, meeting in the center of her forehead.

God smiles on fools and idiots, though, because I was saved from having to respond when my Great-Uncle Alberto, Nonna's youngest brother, announced, "The padre is here."

As a unit, every head turned toward the elevator where—God help me—Fr. Mario alighted, ecumenically garbed in his supreme unction cassock, complete with a crucifix dropped around his neck and a purple stole across his shoulders draped down over his torso like a scarf, signifying to every Catholic in the know he was visiting a sick parishioner.

Again, I swear if I didn't have bad luck, I'd have no luck, because the first person his eyes focused on was me.

Like the lyrics in an old 1950s song, I had nowhere to run to, baby, nowhere to hide.

His face was pinched and tight, like he needed to have a good bowel movement sometime soon. He glared at me while making his way over to where I was still holding Mama.

I said a silent prayer to St. Jude Thaddeus, the patron saint of lost causes, for help. The last thing I needed was for Fr. Mario to question me about my church-confession defection in front of almost my entire living family.

St. Jude heard my plea and yanked Mama from my

arms and toward the good father.

Thanking him profusely for coming on such short notice, she guided him to the room Uncle Vito had called home, lo these many years.

I let out the breath I hadn't realized I'd been holding and leaned up against a wall.

The sound of sobbing had almost turned to white noise for me when a sudden loud cry careened through the hallway, followed by copious shouts and wails.

I took this to mean Uncle Vito had left us for his heavenly reward, verified when a nun wearing a nursing cap in place of her wimple and a white apron over her habit, exited his room, her hands together in prayer, her lips moving silently.

The thing about Italians is, no matter how much we fight, argue, or don't speak to one another for decades, when someone leaves this world, we mourn.

And we mourn big.

Uncle Vito's little corner of the world got much smaller in the next few minutes as most of the relatives present packed into his room like a tin of fresh flash-frozen sardines. The family collectively made the sign of the cross with Fr. Mario leading the way.

After he said a solemn prayer for Vito's soul—he truly was good at his vocation, despite his perpetual, grumpy demeanor—the women in the room took turns kissing Vito's cheek.

There are some traditions common to Catholics and Italians I love. Big weddings, even bigger baptisms, Sunday-after-church family dinners, families all living within walking distance of one another, homemade pasta and red sauce.

These things fill me with happiness and joy.

The one tradition and practice I absolutely hate with every ounce of my being is the *l'addio bacio,* the kiss good-bye. This barbaric ritual of kissing a dead person on the lips or the cheek is just too icky for me and always has been since Nonna made me kiss Nonno when he passed on.

The doctors said my grandfather died from a failed heart. My daddy swore the man had been browbeaten to death by his wife.

"Fifty-plus years of marriage to the *vecchia strega* (old witch, Chloe translated for me) and he finally gave up and gave in. God rest his soul."

Nonno's was the first family death I can remember, and at D'Pierreli's Funeral Parlor, Nonna had taken my shaking hand and brought me up to the casket.

"Kiss him good-bye," she commanded.

I remember I stared down at the coffin, at this figure who looked nothing like my old and gray grandfather, and a sudden uncontrollable urge to pee shot through me. This always happened when I got scared as a kid.

Nonno's eyes were closed, his cheeks had what looked like his wife's face powder across them, and his lips were an unnatural deep pink tone, not the blue-tinged, oxygen-depleted color I was used to seeing. From the corners of his mouth, I spied two strings, which I later learned from Chloe were thread to keep his mouth sewn shut.

"Go on," Nonna insisted.

I swear I was going to wet my pants any second, so to get this over with, I leaned into the casket, scrunched my eyes tightly closed, puckered my lips, and kissed him somewhere in the vicinity of his right ear.

At just that second, the first trickle of warm, sticky

urine dropped into my underpants. I made a mad dash to the bathroom, Chloe following behind.

So when I tell you I hate the *l'addio bacio* tradition with a passion, you can believe me.

I was able to avoid kissing Uncle Vito due to the large number of people present in his room. I simply got lost in the crowd and just pretended I'd kissed him when in reality I never even got close to the bed.

I also managed to avoid getting cornered by Fr. Mario by volunteering to escort Nonna home while my mother and father dealt with the necessary paperwork for the nursing home and the funeral parlor. I grabbed Nonna's arm and hustled her into the elevator, all the while feeling Fr. Mario's intense, distrustful stare burning through my back.

In the cab ride home, Nonna was silent. I sat next to her, her withered, aged hand woven into mine, and noticed how cold it was without her gloves. I tried to rub some warmth into it with my fingers and got a silent squeeze for my efforts.

Nonna didn't talk much on any given day. She really didn't have to because she had a black belt in kinesthesia. Her daughters were good at relaying what they wanted or thought about something with simple shrugs and eye rolls, but Nonna was the true grandmaster of the practice.

One askance glance, or just one eyelid moving to half-open while her gaze zeroed in on you, was enough to put fear into the mightiest of warriors.

"I'm going to bed," she said in the language of her homeland the moment we got through the door, suddenly looking all of her ninety-three years. "Tell your mama I'll help her with everything in the morning."

She kissed my forehead and rubbed a gnarled, craggy finger down my cheek. *"Mi brava ragazza, Gia."* My good girl. *"Te amo."*

"I love you, too, Nonna."

And I did, in spite of the cantankerous way she acted and the rude way she treated people. In truth, she was an excellent female role model: strong, loyal, and fiercely protective.

Plus, one heck of a good cook.

After my parents came home, exhausted and emotionally drained, I kissed them good night and as I settled into bed, said a prayer for Uncle Vito's soul and several for me to help me figure out what to do about the situation with Santini, because despite my best effort, I still hadn't been absolved of my sins or actions.

Chapter Seven

Morning came and with it, relatives from far and near.

By nine a.m., the house was packed with people who'd come to help plan Uncle Vito's funeral and start the official mourning rituals.

Nonna and Mama had been up since four, baking and baking and baking some more. On any given day, the aromas emanating from within my house were enough to cause strangers walking by our brownstone to stop, sniff the air, and sigh with pleasure. Mama made most of what we ate from scratch, forgoing boxed mixes, jarred sauces, and canned vegetables. Today, my home smelled absolutely mouthwatering.

Yards of fresh bread, dozens of sweet cakes and muffins, three of Mama's prize-winning coffee cakes made with the secret ingredient she shared with no one she hadn't given birth to filled the kitchen and spilled out into the dining room.

And even though these two little women had been up cooking enough for an army and a half since before the light cracked the dawn, people still brought food with them.

How to be a Good Italian, Lesson Five:
Never, ever arrive at someone's house
without a gift. And a food gift is always best.

Most of the people who showed up on our doorstep

this morning brought something from Pontevecchio's Paneterria, knowing what a family favorite the items from the bakery were.

I had a busy day ahead of me with another late-morning test downtown and then the scheduled shift at our booth at the fair.

No one forgot today was the first day of the St. Rita's Christmas Festival, least of all Mama. Chloe was slotted to be the official booth opener, with my Aunt Gracie relieving her at noon. I'd be there by three and work until nine tonight. It was a long day, but if Uncle Vito hadn't up and died, Mama and Nonna would have worked at least ten of the twelve hours it was scheduled to be open.

Before I left to catch the downtown train, Mama pulled me aside and wound my scarf around my neck to ward off the evil chill that had blown through and settled during the night. "I'm gonna have Daddy put a few cases of sauce into my car before he leaves for work. Chloe's got some, but hopefully we'll need more for later. When you get home, you take my car to the festival. I'm sure someone will be there to help you unload."

I said a silent prayer it wouldn't be a certain soon-to-be-ordained priest.

She knotted my scarf at the ends and kissed my cheek.

"I'm sorry I can't help with the funeral arrangements." I hugged her. Traces of cinnamon, nutmeg, yeast, and Shalimar drifted up to me and filled my mind with a familiar peace and calm.

Like she was swatting an annoying fly, Mama slapped her hand into the air.

"Don't be. There are enough of us to get everything taken care of. Since Nonna is the oldest one of them alive now"—she made the sign of the cross—"all the final decisions will be hers. You just do good on your test and don't worry about anything here. I'll see you later."

I kissed her good-bye, crossed myself in front of the pontiff's picture, and left.

****

"Your sister had a slow start," Aunt Gracie told me when I showed up at St. Rita's parking lot later that afternoon. "But business picked up around one, and we sold out the first case."

The electronic cigarette perpetually hanging from the corner of her mouth for the past three months glowed amber in the fading and cloudy afternoon light.

I shoved one more case of family sauce at her and then retrieved the other from where I'd parked the car.

The festival was pretty crowded for early afternoon, but it was the first day. By six tonight, it would be even more so and in full first-night swing when the working parishioners brought their families out. The local Scouts were grilling hotdogs, hamburgers, and sundry other fast foods at their booth for parents who didn't want to cook dinner. The Italian club, the men's organization from the neighborhood, of which Daddy is the treasurer, had sausage and peppers available for sale to boost the club's coffers. The local Y had an information booth, and the volunteers staffing it were giving out free granola bars. St. Rita's Elementary School booth was staffed with kids and their parents offering popcorn, red- and green-colored cotton candy, and fried dough for sale.

As predicted, the nuns of St. Rita's were going strong with Christmas card sales, even though the big day was only two weeks away and most people had already mailed this year's cards.

"I bought two boxes for next year." Aunt Gracie cocked her head toward the nuns, her fake cigarette swaying precariously from between her lips.

I recognized many of the people ambling and milling around, browsing at the sale huts, and giving Christmas good wishes to neighbors.

I loved this festival. Even as a kid, I enjoyed walking around and taking in the sights of all the craft booths and smells of the foods offered for sale. Chloe and I had purchased many a Christmas gift for our parents and Nonna here when we were younger and had only babysitting and allowance money to spend. Mama still uses a decoupage jewelry box Chloe gave her one year, and she wears an angel pin I gave her on her coat every year during Christmas season.

"Look, Gia baby"—Gracie took a huge drag on her make-believe cigarette—"I think you'll be okay on your own. I wanna get back to the house and see how everything's comin' along with the plans."

I nodded and told her to go. I would be fine.

In truth, being around Aunt Gracie is kind of exhausting. She never stops talking—*never*—and she asks questions as fast as they pop into her head, without giving you any time to answer. Topics and discussions roll off and out of her at a whim, and I usually get a subtle headache whenever I'm around her.

I love her, like I love all my aunts and uncles, but she can be trying on my soul and my patience.

For the next two hours, I sold a total of three jars of

sauce, chatted with a few of the nuns, and watched families enjoy themselves.

At five, when it started moving from twilight into full night, I turned on our Christmas lights, causing a domino effect around the parking lot. I said a silent prayer to God, thanking him for helping Uncle Sonny come through with flying colors this time.

Uncle Sonny needs all the prayers he can get to offset so many of his ethical demerits.

I took a little bit of pride at how great the huts looked all lit up. Mama had gotten a uniformity of white lights, not the standard Christmas-tree-colored red and green ones you'd expect, and because of the bright color, the parking lot looked angelic and holy, which was a good thing considering it was a church Christmas festival.

Thinking about how long it had taken to string the lights got me to thinking about the person who'd helped me.

I was still overcome with conflicting and tormenting emotions at what had happened between us. It's one thing to have lusty fantasies about a guy. Quite another to actually act on them.

I still couldn't reconcile my diverse and quicksilver emotions whenever I was in Santini's presence. One minute I wanted to jump him, his utter sexiness driving me insane; the next, I didn't feel anything out of the ordinary. Once again I looked deep inside myself, pondering on whether I was experiencing some weird kind of seasonal mood affect disorder or behavioral syndrome. Test stress, holiday stress, just-living-with-a-crazy-family stress could all lead to some kind of emotional collapse, couldn't it?

Chloe's husband, Matt, is a doctor, and I knew I could seek out his advice on the matter. But Matt is a direct pipeline to Chloe, and I was certain I didn't want her to know what I'd done. She'd love me no matter what dumb or ridiculous situation I'd gotten myself into, but I just wasn't open to her finding out the way I'd acted with a man of the cloth. There had to be a special room in hell for people like me, and I just knew I was heading there.

Chloe texted me once to ask if I was okay at the booth alone, and I responded I was, no worries. Not two minutes later Mama texted asking me the same thing, and I returned the text telling her she should talk with Chloe. That started a messaging war, where she immediately shot back asking me what was wrong. Why should she talk to Chloe when she could talk to me? Was I hungry? Did I need a break? Was I dressed warmly enough? Yada, yada, yada.

Sometimes I wish my parents hadn't moved into the twenty-first century and learned about e-mail, texting, and smart phones. Life was a lot easier in my house when they were tech-*NO*-savvy and used the old rotary phone Nonna still had hooked up in her room.

By seven thirty, I'd had ten texts from Mama and I needed a bathroom break. Miraculously, just when I considered closing the booth for a few minutes to run into the church and relieve myself, Daddy showed up with a shopping bag.

"Your mama thought you might be getting hungry by now." He dropped a kiss on my head. "So I volunteered to bring you a little something to eat."

"You didn't need to, Daddy, but thanks."

"In truth, Gia baby, I needed to get outta the house."

His sigh was deep, guttural, and filled with meaning. "Nonna's driving everyone to drink with the funeral arrangements. Before it came to blows, I figured I'd hightail it outta there and get some air."

"Hold on, Daddy," I said, sliding under the door divider, thrilled I could get a bathroom break. "I'll be back in five."

It was a little more than the five minutes I'd predicted before I got back. The line for the ladies' room in the church was twenty deep, and there were only two operational stalls in use. The rest had been roped off using yellow crime-scene tape. I knew no actual crime had been committed, or anything gruesome had occurred. The bathroom was being updated, and Dottie Allegari's husband was a cop, so he'd donated the tape to keep people from using the toilets before the maintenance was completed. It did look weird, though.

Relieved, truly, I made my way back to our booth, ready to dive into Mama's care bag, when I stopped dead in my tracks by the nun hut.

Daddy was leaning against the open window frame of our booth, speaking with the last person on earth I wanted to see. Fr. Santini.

Dressed in his full priestly regalia this evening, he had on bright green woolen mittens that looked handmade and a matching skullcap covering his ears against the chilly December night air.

They were engrossed in conversation and hadn't noticed me approaching, so I did the cowardly thing and shot around to the side of the hut so I wouldn't be seen.

Again, if I didn't have bad luck, I'd have none, because my desire to go unseen fizzled fast.

"Gia Gabriella, is something wrong?" Sister Alberta

Frances, my third grade teacher, old as the hills when I was in her class, asked when she spotted me skulking. Sister Alberta Frances loved names. All names. And she called her students by their full first and second ones. I was lucky she hadn't taught sixth grade when we made confirmation. Then she would have addressed me as Gia Gabriella Bernadetta. It would have taken forever to call the roll in class every day. As it was with just two names per student, it had taken a chunk of each morning.

"Nothing's wrong, Sister." I planted a smile on my face and hoped I didn't look guilty from fibbing. "I just don't want to interrupt Daddy when he's talking with the new gu—er, with Fr. Santini."

Sister Alberta Frances peered at me through her cataract glasses. Her eyes were huge from the magnification she needed, the left one permanently drifting outward from a congenital defect—so whenever she looked straight at you, you were never sure you were what she was truly looking at—and filled with the skepticism only a sister of a holy order can pull off.

Out of the corner of my eye, I saw Santini glance my way, and I quickly plastered myself to the side of the hut, trying to make myself invisible and not thinking about what I was doing.

I say that because if I *had* been thinking, I would never have leaned up against the wooden enclosure clad in the thick wool sweater I had on. The second I flattened myself against the plank, I felt a giant tug around my mid-back.

Yup, you guessed it. My sweater snagged on an errant sticking-out splinter of wood. Not thinking—again—I yanked back and heard a jagged ripping sound. Cold air immediately permeated the skin at my back.

The rip was somewhere around the bottom of my bra strap, so I couldn't see it. I tried to get a feel for it by slipping my hand over my head and then trying to reach it from below, but my arm was too short both ways. I know I looked like some kind of crazy-ass contortionist as I flapped my arm up and then down several times, trying to disengage myself, shaking my shoulders right and left in a vain attempt to reach the tear. You see, the sweater had ripped, but it hadn't disengaged from the wood chunk, and I was still stuck to the plank—or my sweater was, which is the same thing because I was wearing it.

Now, this whole time, Sister Alberta watched me doing my awkward, flapping, disengagement dance, squinting through her Mr. Magoo magnifying glasses, without offering any help.

And I needed help. I knew if I tugged one more time, the sweater would probably rend in half and fall off my body. I didn't relish being seen by the entire festival clad in my black lace bra.

"Sister, do you think you can give me a hand here? I'm stuck." I hoped the subtle whine and pleading tone in my voice would be of benefit.

She was cut off from whatever it was she was going to say to me when Daddy called out, "Gia baby. Come over here and say hello to the new padre."

My heart froze to icicle status inside my chest.

Caught. So much for trying to remain invisible.

"Just a sec, Daddy," I called. To Alberta, "Sister? Can you help me?"

With a head bobble I took for a nod, she moved behind me and groped around on the plank. Because it was full-dark nighttime and the huts were lit in the front, not the side or back, she didn't have a very good view of where I was hung up, so she had to feel her way around my back.

Do you know how uncomfortable it is to be felt up by a nun? It's not pleasant, that's for sure.

Cataract surgery couldn't come quick enough for Sister Alberta.

After a moment or two, she managed to snake her arthritic, gnarled hands around the snag and pushed the patch of sweater caught in it up and off. I was able to move again, but my back was freezing. I couldn't imagine how huge the hole was. I'd planned ahead, though, thinking it might be cold during the evening hours, so I had a down vest back at our booth.

I thanked the good sister for her help.

"I'll say a prayer for you, Gia Gabriella." She adjusted her glasses and peered at me through them, as if looking at a new life form under a microscope. "Maybe more than one."

In all truth, I could use all the help I could get.

Like a heretic on her way to the gallows during the Inquisition, I shuffled my way back over to our booth.

Daddy wrapped one arm around my shoulders and gave me a squeeze as he introduced me. I was surprised he couldn't feel how my entire body was shaking from nerves at seeing Fr. Santini, and because of the big-time hole in the back of my sweater letting in the chilly night air.

"This is the baby in my family, Father. Gia. Gia, say hello to Fr. Santini."

I reached back and grabbed my vest off a folding chair and tugged it on, zipping it all the way up to my neck. Done, I looked at Santini.

I guess I expected him to say something like, "Oh, we met on setup day," but he didn't. He smiled down at me, removed a mitten, and stuck out his hand. "Your father's been telling me all about how hard you've been studying for your exams."

We shook hands, his pumping mine enthusiastically, not a trace of acknowledgement his eyes.

Now here's the really weird thing. I mean, aside from the fact he basically just committed a sin of omission by denying he knew me. Yesterday in the park, the minute he put his hand on my arm a jolt of electricity surged through my clothes and my system like a lightning bolt, settling in my soul, heating my whole body, and making my girlie parts shake like uncooked *scungille*.

But right now, with my bare hand settled into his, skin against skin with no barrier, there was absolutely nothing. Not a twinge. Not a jolt. Not a bead of awareness. The beautiful chaos of colors in his eyes as he gazed down at me did nothing to my insides. Not a quake. Not a quiver. Not a trickle of lust.

What. The. H. E. Double hockey sticks was going on?

This was the guy I'd wrapped my tongue around twenty-four hours ago and practically climbed up on just to get closer to. The man I'd—God forgive my soul—dry-humped in broad daylight.

In public.

Daddy squeezed me again. "I tell ya, Father, she's the bright spot in my day."

Fr. Santini smiled down at me, and again I was filled with confusion. His smile looked a little different, a little...well...smaller than I remembered. And it did nothing to my insides. No zippidee-do-da feeling. No desire to scream "Take me, I'm yours."

Nothing.

Like I said, weird.

He'd slipped his funky-colored gloves back on after shaking hands.

I don't know what possessed me, but before I could stop myself I said, "Nice hat and mittens."

I heard the sarcasm in my voice, but apparently no one else did, because Fr. Santini's face lit up like an LED light.

"My sister, Elizabeth Ann, made them for me last Christmas. In fact, she made them for all my siblings."

"Elizabeth Ann," Daddy said, "is the one who's special needs, right, Padre? I remember you saying that at mass."

"Yes. She's the love of my family, too. I've never met a happier, sweeter kid. She's simply a delight to be around."

Awww. That was just too sweet. What a great brother. I remembered he'd said pretty much the same thing in Pontevecchio's about his sister. I said a silent prayer for the parking lot to open again so I could hop on that express to hell, where I so deserved to go.

Addressing Daddy and looking around, the father said, "This turnout is wonderful. It's great to see so many parishioners involved in the festival."

"St. Rita's is a close-knit parish, Father. You'll see, once you're all settled in. We're like a big family. Like yours." Daddy looked down at me. "Remember the father is one of ten kids, Gia? He was telling us about his family during his homily."

I nodded, not correcting him about my whereabouts during mass. I didn't want to remind him about Arianna's gastric explosion. It didn't seem like appropriate conversation in front of a priest.

But as always, I forgot my family doesn't hold back on whether something is appropriate or not.

"Oh, wait. You missed that." Daddy smacked his palm across his forehead. "My new granddaughter," he said to the priest, "needed her diaper changed. Stunk up the entire section. Who knew something so little could be so packed with foul-smelling stuff?"

He laughed, and I wanted the earth to open up and drop me down to hell ASAP.

"Gia is Arianna's godmother, so she did the honors of changing her. Missed your introduction."

"My sister Mary Alice just had a baby a month ago," Fr. Santini said with a grin. "Her third girl. I'm used to being around little ones since I'm an uncle five times over." His smile grew wider. "I'm finally going to get to baptize one, too. I'm officiating at little Sophia's ceremony on New Year's, right after my ordination."

Daddy smiled, said "Congrats," and crossed himself.

Reflexively, I did the same.

The two of them continued speaking while I just stood there, silently seething and so uncomfortable I wanted to scream.

How could he act as if nothing had happened between us? And forgetting all about the kiss, because, of course, he wouldn't want to tell my father he'd had his tongue down my throat, his strong hands cupping my butt, why hadn't he admitted we'd met on setup day? We'd spent quite some time together, and he never even acknowledged it.

Why not?

All this ran through my head while they spoke. I was beginning to get an Aunt Gracie-like headache when I was pulled away by someone wanting to buy a few jars of sauce. Thrilled for the diversion, I gladly took care of the sale.

"I'll have my wife call the rectory soon, Padre, and set up a time you can join my family for dinner," Daddy said as Fr. Santini walked away from our booth.

What?

When Santini was out of earshot, I turned on my father. "Why did you invite him to dinner? He can't possibly come to our house."

Daddy's bushy eyebrows pulled together, making him look like he had two caterpillars crawling on his forehead. "Why not?" Concern tugged his mouth down. "Your mama specifically told me to ask him if I saw him here tonight."

There was no way I could tell him the real reason the good father should never be allowed in our home. If Daddy ever found out a priest had kissed me, and not in a pure, innocent, holy manner, and I'd been a willing participant in the encounter, well, Uncle Sonny would be calling some of his nefarious friends to make a St. Rita's run at midnight and we'd never see the young padre again.

Ever.

"I just mean he'll be too busy getting used to the parish to take time out to visit and have supper. He's new. He needs to attend to parish business, not visit with people. Help Fr. Mario, now that he's here. You know...do priest things and...stuff."

Mio Dio. This babbling was becoming an uncomfortable habit.

Daddy continued to stare at me, his frown deepening, the groves folding down his cheeks like craters imploding. "When was the last time you ate something, Gia? 'Cuz your brain isn't working too good right now. You're talking all weird and disconnected. Here." He handed me Mama's care bag. "You need some food. Eat the snack Mama sent."

How to be a Good Italian, Lesson Six:
When something emotional comes up, eat.
Without a doubt, it is the only way
to deal with the problem effectively.

So I did.

Chapter Eight

Burying someone right before Christmas is a tricky endeavor. The churches are decorated for the joyous holiday, not a funeral procession, draped in virginal white, not despondent black. Bright red poinsettias fill the altar, not stark, frost-colored lilies of the valley. The Christmas season instills in one and all a sense of happiness at Jesus's birth, not sadness at a mortal's passing.

But Uncle Vito needed to be waked and buried no matter what time of year he left us for his heavenly reward, and Nonna made sure her older brother went out in the style befitting a fallen son of Italy.

And by that I mean she pulled out all the stops and spared no expense. Or I should say she spared none of Daddy's expense, since he was the one footing the bill. How that happened I have no idea.

We waked Uncle Vito in the Mogliadini Family Funeral Home on Thursday and Friday. Nonna had insisted her brother be laid out in the Cadillac of the viewing rooms, affectionately called the Eternal Reward Parlor. It was twice as big as the other viewing rooms and was the most aesthetically pleasing to the eye, according to Nonna. Rich, dark cherrywood paneling lined the walls; a floor-to-ceiling bay window on one side overlooked the East River; numerous capo diamanté cherubim and seraphim statues were scattered around the room on pedestals. Portraits of the last three Holy Fathers framed the walls, in addition to two humongous oil depictions of a crucified Christ.

In my opinion the room was fourteen kinds of creepy, but whatever Nonna wants, Nonna gets.

So.

Eternal Reward was packed to the mourning rafters both nights. Cousins—first, second, and third—showed up to pay their respects, some of whom I hadn't seen since I was a kid or had never even met.

The room exploded with people, flowers, and floral arrangements, the largest from Uncle Vito's old OTB gambling cronies. An obscenely massive assortment of red and pink lilies, carnations, and roses, it had a six-foot gold banner with "He played the odds and won big. Happy travels wherever you wind up, Vito" across it.

Nonna's face pinched into her constipated-and-needing-relief look when she spied it standing in a place of honor next to the coffin. She clicked her tongue, slithered her eyelids down to almost closing, and mumbled something under her breath in Italian.

I wouldn't have been surprised if she'd put a curse on the whole gang of them.

As good little Italians, we all wore black, although the only ones to be totally decked out from underclothes to outerwear were the relatives who were eighty and above, this being a sign of high respect for the departed. Very old-school Italian and old-world traditional. Nonna dressed head to toe in black every day of her life, so she looked just like she always did.

I won't bore you with all the over-the-top stories and remembrances about Vito that passed those two nights between his relatives and betting buddies. Suffice it to say I got a little queasy when tales of his rumored sexual prowess were discussed by the cronies, all of them laughing, then wheezing from laughing, and then choking from wheezing.

I was prepared a couple of times for one of them to keel over from lack of oxygen. In fact, the owner of Vito's favorite OTB parlor arrived attached to an oxygen tank he wheeled in front of him. He had the loudest laugh/wheeze of all.

Mama instructed me to stick close to Nonna while she *received* the mourners and to make sure she had everything she needed, like tissues, memorial cards, water. In truth, Mama wanted me to keep an eye out for any signs my grandmother was getting ready to let loose and go postal on the relatives.

Don't laugh…there's been precedent.

At Nonno's visitation, two of his surviving brothers arrived three-sheets-to-the-wind smashed, having spent the afternoon toasting him at a local bar. And by *toasting*, I mean doing shots. A lot of shots. The brothers were loud, obnoxious, and annoying during the somber service, saying inappropriate things and laughing at each other's silly jokes. Nonna, the bereaved widow, had taken a fireplace poker and brandished it like a sword, expelling them from the wake.

So when Mama asked me to stick close it was because, as the youngest grandchild, I'm also the quickest.

Mogliadini's was stifling and overheated from the crush of bodies present both nights. The heat was jacked up high because it was winter, but it was unnecessary since the throng of people throwing off body heat would have been sufficient to boil an egg. Everyone who came to pay respects stayed until viewing hours were over.

There's no such thing at an Italian wake as simply paying your respects and then leaving.

No such luck.

Every mourner arrived right on time—if not fifteen minutes early to claim a space in line—paraded in front of the decedent's coffin, said a prayer, and then delivered a few words of condolence to the immediate family.

This is where most people would now exit.

Not my relatives.

Every last one of them claimed a folding chair as their own or else crowded around the perimeter of the room, watching, noting, and assessing every other mourner.

And also commenting on Uncle Vito: how he looked, the circumstances of his death, and what was going to happen to his estate since he never married and had apparently—according to one fourth cousin I overheard talking and whom I didn't know from Adam—socked away his race-track winnings all his life to leave one tidy nest egg.

All agreed he looked too young to have died. Ninety-six, they concurred, and he appeared no older than eighty.

On my way to get Nonna more water because she was literally wilting from the heat, I eavesdropped on a pair of fifty-something fringe relatives as they were discussing how Vito died.

Fringe relative #1: So sad to go out the way he did.

FR #2: How?

FR #1: Didn't you hear? *Gesu.* They found him sitting up in his bed, covered in his own waste, a big whopping infection in his urine no one knew he had. Temperature of one hundred and six. Disgraceful.

FR# 2: *Madonna*. Think we can sue?

Remember that body language I told you Mama is a pro at? These two had the same moves. Fringe relative number one put her hands palms up, frowned, shot her eyebrows up her forehead, and shrugged. "Who knows?"

I was so tempted to stop and tell them the plain, sad truth. Vito died when an all-consuming stroke shook through his weakened system, shutting off the necessary volume of blood and oxygen his heart and brain needed.

He didn't have an infection, and he hadn't been found lying in bed covered in poop and pee.

At the time he'd stroked, he'd been sitting in his wheelchair, strapped in with a chest restraint so he wouldn't fall out, reruns of *I Love Lucy* playing on the big-screen television mounted on the wall.

Italians do love their drama, though.

Suffice it to say I neglected telling any of this to Nonna, fearful she'd grab the closest pointed object she could find and wield it at them.

****

Saturday morning, we laid Vito to rest in St. Rita's cemetery.

The day was cold and clear, a steady wind pulling off the East River as Vito was placed into the family grave next to three brothers and a sister who beat him to heaven.

Ten days before Christmas is not a bustling time for burials. The ground is winter-frozen hard, the work of opening it up for casket placement, tough and arduous. I'd heard Daddy whisper to Mama just the night before that Uncle Sonny had to call in some markers just so we'd have good gravediggers on hand and not some inebriated holiday part-timer fly-by-nights who wouldn't do as good a job.

Fr. Mario officiated at the mass, Fr. Heartthrob, as I'd taken to calling him, by his side.

I hadn't seen the good almost-priest since the first night of the festival. Chloe's husband, Matt, and my brothers' wives had been working at the family booth in shifts during the week so immediate *blood* family—and Nonna had been insistent on using *that* word—could help her plan for Uncle Vito's wake and funeral. The entire family, though, was present for the wake, mass, and burial.

Italians are amazing cooks, artists, architects, and carmakers. What we do best in my opinion, though, is mourn.

We are not shy about showing our soul-sucking emotions, men and women alike. And when we are mourning a family member, well, that's when we shine like the gold lacing the dome of St. Peter's Basilica.

Nonna and her remaining brothers and their wives sat in the front row in church, Mama and her sisters and brothers included. I was two rows back, behind my father, brothers, and their families, holding Arianna and sitting next to Chloe and her family.

The church reeked of acrid-smelling incense as the good fathers swung the thurible back and forth across the altar and then over Uncle Vito's closed casket, creating an incense smoke storm over the front of the church. This was the one part of any mass I hated. I always stank of frankincense and cloves for the rest of the day, no amount of fresh air or perfume helping to mask the powerful odor.

Lorenzo was squirming in his seat next to his father, holding his nose, his mouth and the corners of his little eyes pulling down into disgusted and expressive two-year-old grimaces.

The smoke billowed into a cloud of noxious vapor, wafting throughout St. Rita's.

Nonna held a handkerchief across her mouth and nose, spritzed with what I knew were a few drops of her favorite old-lady perfume, as pungent and overpowering as the burning spices and resins.

Every few moments a sob or a loud sniffle would drown out Fr. Mario's metronomic delivery of the mass. I knew this was just the buildup to what was coming. By the time Uncle Vito's soul was blessed and sent on its way to heaven—or wherever it was headed—the wailing and keening would start, big time. Family members who hadn't seen him in years would be prostrating themselves on one another, crying about what a good man he was and how could he leave us when he had so much still to live for, when he was still such a vital man?

Obviously, they'd forgotten the past few years of his life, secured to a chair by a chest restraint so he wouldn't fall to the floor and break a hip, a plastic catheter attached to his shriveled and unused manhood, and a feeding tube draining into his stomach.

But he still had so much to live for, they'd say. Even at ninety-six.

Italians…

Arianna was sound asleep in my arms, her little newborn snores and baby body noises charming and delighting me as I rocked her gently. I snuck a glance at

Chloe, her hand held in her good-looking, successful husband's grip, a look of utter love and contentment across her face.

The truth is I wanted the same thing in my life. A man who adored me beyond reason, children I could hold and coddle and spoil, and a love that lasted forever.

My gaze drifted up to the altar. Fr. Santini, handsome and resplendent in his somber ceremonial robes, was preparing for Communion.

I was still reeling from the way he'd so easily disregarded what had happened between us, and I'd been deliberating the past few days if I should say something to him about it, in private.

But in saying something, I had to admit culpability as well, something I didn't want to do.

How was it possible I could look at him one day and be so overcome by desire I couldn't put a sentence together, and the next day, it was as if we were strangers just meeting?

Something was obviously wrong with me. Exam stress, family commotion, my worries about my future…something. There was no logical way I could explain the dichotomy of my emotions and actions. I seriously considered making an appointment with our family doctor and scheduling a mental wellness checkup, but I nixed the idea almost the moment it bloomed because our family doc is the son of an old friend of one of Nonna's Rosary Society members. You might think, *so what*? But believe me when I tell you in Italian culture there is no such thing as obeying federally mandated privacy laws. The information superhighway can trace its origins straight back to little-old-Italian-lady *caffè* klatches. If I went for a psych evaluation, the entire neighborhood and parish would know about it before I left the shrink's office.

When Communion came, I lifted Arianna and followed the procession. The church was packed with family, some of Vito's ambulatory, non-brain-fried friends from the nursing home, and a large number of his old betting buddies and cohorts, so both priests were charged with giving Communion.

I was happy I was on Fr. Mario's side of the aisle. I didn't know if I could look Santini in the eyes again and not blush or give away what I'd been thinking.

As predicted, as soon as the mass drew to a close and the priests blessed the coffin, Vito's soul, etc., the yowling and wailing started. Arianna gave a little slumberous, unconscious jump in my arms when one of the third—or possibly fourth—cousins screeched Vito's name in grief-stricken reverence.

How to be a Good Italian, Lesson Seven:
Show the world your true emotions.
Never hold back.

Two members of the Moglidiani family wheeled Vito's coffin out of the church, behind the priests, the incense wafting in the air like pot at a college kegger, and placed it in the waiting hearse.

All the mourners piled into the ten limos Nonna had insisted we hire to ferry us to the cemetery. Daddy balked at the unnecessary expense, but as usual Uncle Sonny knew a guy who knew a guy who ran a limo service, so we got "a great deal" on the rentals. As we'd been divvied up in the church, we were again in the limousines, with me, thankfully, with Chloe's clan.

The drive took a mere five minutes, and then once again we all met as a unit and surrounded the open grave, the casket on risers, waiting to be lowered. The cold December breeze had a decided icy bite to it. One of the Moglidiani brothers handed white roses to each mourner as we gathered around the casket.

Chairs were set up in front of the open plot for the oldest members. Nonna elected to stand, clinging to Mama's arm for support for once, instead of mine. She was bundled up, wooly hat to sensible shoes, in somber black. Of all of us, she looked the toastiest, garbed as she was against the frigid day.

When we were all graveside, we bowed our heads as Fr. Mario led us in one last prayer.

After he finished, we were each encouraged to approach the closed casket, say a silent prayer or a good-bye, and then toss the rose on the top of the coffin, which would be lowered into the ground once we exited the cemetery.

The caterwauling started up again, louder and more intense than during the church service, as the mourners made their way to the grave. I fully expected one of the geriatric set to throw themselves onto the casket.

Don't laugh. Again, I can cite precedent.

Nonna, of course, remained her stoic, always composed self, but she darted squinty-eyed, *malocchio*-filled glares at the more bombastic of her relatives.

In my twenty-four years, I had never seen my grandmother cry. Not once. Not when her husband died and she'd forced me to kiss his cold, lifeless cheek. Not when her oldest son was killed in a car crash by a drunken driver. Not when her favorite sister succumbed to her hard-fought battle against colon cancer.

After ninety-three years, five global wars, poverty, immigration, ten children, and too many family tragedies to name, Constanza Maria Louisia D'Paolo Chiccolini had seen enough to be immune to grief-filled tears.

The one tradition my family didn't partake in during burials was waiting and viewing the coffin as it was lowered into the ground. This, to me, was the final, heartbreaking good-bye, and I couldn't bear it. Neither could anyone else, so we were escorted back to our cars and taken back to my parents' home before the interment.

The street in front of our house looked like a holding company for shiny black limousines. Alighting from ours, Lorenzo's hand in hers, Chloe quipped, "Think the neighbors will assume Uncle Sonny got a great deal on a new fleet of family cars?"

Laughing felt good after the doleful way we'd spent the morning.

Inside the house, food awaited, and for once, Mama had allowed the majority of it to be catered instead of slaving away in the kitchen making enough to feed our army of relations.

Per custom, Frs. Mario and Santini had been invited back to the house. I said a silent prayer of thanks to St. Gregory of Neocaesarea, the patron saint of wonderworks, for keeping the younger padre occupied at St. Rita's. I knew I could keep out of Fr. Mario's way during the postburial gathering, but I wasn't all together certain I could avoid them both.

Mama and the aunts took over the kitchen, organizing the food distribution, heating up things that needed heating, and generally making sure all the food ordered had arrived as requested. Mama asked me to continue to keep an eye on Nonna, but it was an easy job, because the moment we walked into the house she'd divested herself of her martyred outwear and plopped down into her favorite chair in the sitting room, feet raised on the ottoman, ready to receive. I brought her a plate filled with food Mama had prepared for her, along with a tumbler filled with her favorite sambuca. She deserved it.

Luckily—and thank you, St. Gregory—I was able to keep Fr. Mario in my line of sight so whenever I sensed him getting close, I shot to the other side of the room, hid behind the Christmas tree, or skulked off to help Mama or Chloe.

And so, as a family, we drank a toast to Uncle Vito's life, his soul, and his memory, and did what Italians do better than everyone else: eat and talk.

Chapter Nine

Sunday, Mama issued me a reprieve, and I didn't have to work at the festival booth. I had my final accounting exam the next morning, and Daddy convinced her it would be more productive if I stayed home and studied. I could have kissed his feet.

The relatives who'd traveled to bury Vito all went back to their homes, and our lives could now get back to some semblance of normal again.

If the San Valentino family could ever be called normal.

All the stress and tension about taking the exam flew from me once I'd done my last calculation. I'd know by the new year if I passed, and when I found out, I was going to start looking with some serious intent for a job. But for now, there was a week until Christmas and I was ready to start enjoying the time. No more tests, Uncle Vito waked and buried—God rest his soul—and the holiday shopping could commence in full.

One week before Christmas and the weather had at long last decided it was time to declare an official start to winter. A frosty arctic blast from our Canadian siblings had the upper northeast of the United States blanketed with a frigid cold front. By rights it should have been called a front, back, and two sides. Swirling winds and chilly temperatures abounded, and still the festival was packed every afternoon and evening until closing time.

Chloe and I were working together at our booth on the Thursday before the twenty-fifth, Mama and Daddy happily taking care of their two youngest grandbabies.

"I feel like I haven't talked to you in forever," Chloe said. She took a huge sip—more like a gulp—of the hot chocolate the nuns had made to warm the gaggle of booth workers on this chilly day.

"It's been a busy couple of weeks." I smiled at the elderly woman who'd just purchased two quarts of sauce as I handed her change back. "My exams, Uncle Vito. This." I slashed my hand in the air, indicating our surroundings. "I feel like I've been going full speed since Thanksgiving."

"No lie." She put her cup down and graced me with the look she was blessed to receive from Mama at birth. Her tell-me-all-your-secrets-or-else stare: eyes narrowed slightly and lasered onto mine, chin pointed downward, head cocked to the right, and lips moist and pursed.

"So," she said, her usual opening when she was about to grill me like a raw hamburger. "What's new in your life? Man-wise?"

I prayed she couldn't see the heat brandishing up my cheeks. I took my own sip of hot chocolate, a diversionary move I realized too late she wasn't going to tolerate.

"Spill, *sorellina*."

I may have been her little sister, but I had my own tricks I could use. "When have I had time for anything lately, especially guys?"

"No one in school you like?"

I shook my head.

"The aunts haven't fixed you up with anyone new?"

"Well…" I shrugged. "Aunt Ursula set me up with Eddie Piscaponi back near Halloween. Remember him?"

Chloe squinted. "Pimply, short kid with red hair? He was in your class in high school, right?"

I nodded. "He works at a nightclub owned by one of Uncle Sonny's friends. He's the bouncer."

"No kidding? He must have grown, 'cause he was always height challenged. Nice, but not exactly a teenage dream."

I told her I'd agreed to meet Eddie for drinks after school one night in Tribeca.

I almost fell off my barstool when he walked in. His hair was still flaming red and his face pockmarked from the cystic acne he'd suffered from as a kid, but that was where the similarity to his teenage self ended. He'd grown about ten inches since high school and stood towering over me at six five. And he'd filled out. Considerably. Like steroid-induced filled out. His arms looked like Popeye's after a can of spinach, and his head continued down to his shoulders without a break where his neck should be.

After fifteen minutes, I was glad I'd only agreed to drinks and not dinner because I couldn't wait to leave the bar.

I'd liked Eddie Piscaponi a whole lot better when he'd been a geeky, skinny, pimply teenager.

The new supersized adult version was obnoxious, narcissistic, and blessed with an amazing ability to be condescending.

Here's an example.

Me: "So you definitely got a gym membership after high school. Ha-ha."

Eddie (with a self-deprecating chuckle): "Yeah.

After getting the crap beat outta me one too many times, I figured I'd start working out, build a little muscle, and maybe I wouldn't be such an easy target."

He peered at me in the bar's mood lighting, eyes squinting, nose crunched up a little. "You know, Gia, you could stand to lift a few pounds, build some muscle of your own. Don't get me wrong. You look okay, but you kinda lack tone."

He wrapped his index finger and thumb around my upper arm and touched them together. All I could think about when I looked down at his huge hand was the last time Mama cooked a ham for Sunday dinner.

"I could set you up with my trainer. He'll whip you into shape in no time. Or even better, I could take you on. Nothing like getting to know somebody better than sharing a little workout, a little body fluids like sweat, and other things, if you know what I mean."

I had a mental flash of those huge hands crushing me alive when he squeezed my arm again.

I practically inhaled my diet soda, smiled, and then seeking a quick escape, shot a look at my phone. "Oops, I'm late. I've got an appointment uptown," I fibbed. "Gotta go. It was nice seeing you again, Eddie. Take care and say hi to your mom for me."

He tried to kiss me, but I'd seen the move coming, so I pretended to drop something, stooped out of the way to *pretend* pick it up, and then snaked around the guy seated next to us and out of Eddie's reach.

"I'll call ya soon." I heard him yell as I went flying out the bar door.

I waved over my shoulder and sent myself a mental reminder to make sure Aunt Ursula hadn't given him my cell number.

"So that's the last date I had," I said to a laughing Chloe.

"*Gesu,* Gia. It's like watching my life repeated through you."

The aunts had been famous—or is it infamous?—for setting Chloe up before she was married with all types of men from bookies to kneecap breakers, or as Uncle Sonny called them, *employed enforcers.* Providentially, Matt showed up in her life at just the right moment so she was now a very happily married Italian girl with two kids, and the aunts had diverted their matchmaking attentions to me.

"Damn." Chloe wiped a laughter tear from her eye. "I was convinced it was a guy making you so distracted lately. I guess my romance radar is off."

Before I could respond, I heard my name. I'd been about to blow on my hot drink and take a sip when I recognized the voice. Because all logical thought flew from my brain, I took a huge gulp and scalded my tongue and the roof of my mouth on the aptly named hot chocolate.

Santini was standing at the divider of our booth, that weird green skullcap on his head, the matching mittens on his hands, watching me burn myself. In a very unladylike move, one which would have earned a head thwacking from Nonna, I spit the hot liquid back into the Styrofoam cup, wiped the trail of it from my lips with the back of my hand, and stared up into a pair of deer-colored eyes.

"Are you okay?" He grabbed my upper arm. My mouth had been scalded from the liquid, but my arm where his hand rested felt burnt to a crisp.

A really hot—and by hot I mean it in a totally erotic

way—crisp.

I nodded and put the cup down.

"Hi," Chloe said to Santini. "I'm Chloe D'Amore, Gia's sister."

He took off a glove and shook the hand she stuck out. "Tim Santini." He smiled at her, then immediately turned his attention back to me. "Do you have a minute?"

I looked over at Chloe. Her face was sixteen different expressions of curious.

"N-no. Sorry. No, I don't. I need to help with sales. We're swamped tonight. Chloe needs me here to help."

Babbling brook, thy name is Gia Gabriella Bernadetta San Valentino.

He glanced around our immediate outside area, as did Chloe. Festival-goers were moseying from hut to hut, smiling, talking, and having a good time. No one was waiting on line outside our booth.

Santini looked back at me, his eyebrows almost kissing in the center of his forehead.

"I'm good," my traitorous sister declared, her gaze ping-ponging between the two of us. "Take a break, Gia. You deserve one. It's okay."

I'm not as good as Nonna in the *malocchio*-throwing department, but I did my best. Chloe ignored my steely, narrowed-eyed glare.

"Gia?" Santini said.

Here's the thing. What could I do that wouldn't make my sister uber-suspicious? If I continued to refuse to go with him, she'd light into me no end about it. Or worse, she'd question Mama about my behavior, and then I'd be done for.

But I was still nervous from my last solo encounter

with the good almost-priest and couldn't trust myself not to say or do something that would embarrass me even more than I already was.

Stay or go? A lousy choice either way.

"Okay. But just for a minute."

I'm such a coward when it comes to being tattled about to Mama.

Santini lifted the shelf divider, and I went through it.

"Let's take a walk," he said, reaching for my hand.

I snatched it back with a force that knocked me back a step. "You can't hold my hand," I whispered, horrified. "People will see."

His eyebrows met in the center of his head again.

"Good evening, Timothy."

"Hi, Sister Agnes." He turned toward her and smiled.

The elderly nun aimed her eyes that saw all at me. "Gia."

"Merry Christmas," I mumbled, wanting the manhole to hell to open again so I could get it over with and just be dropped where I belonged.

"Are you enjoying your first St. Rita's festival, Timothy?"

"Yes, Sister. I haven't had much of a chance to visit every booth yet because my work schedule has been nuts. But I'm planning to."

Sister Agnes nodded and turned her attention to me. "Your aunt Grace was telling me you're all done with your licensing exams, Gia."

"Yes, Sister, I am."

"Well, I'm sure you did well. You were always a wonder in my classes."

She should know since she'd been my sixth- and seventh-grade math teacher. In fact, she was the first teacher to encourage my math abilities, giving me extra work to do to help me skip ahead. As soon as she recognized my natural ability for numbers, she did everything she could to enhance and support my math skills. Sister Agnes was the person, in fact, who put the drive in me to aim for an occupation where I could use my talents, and for that I'll be eternally thankful.

Right now all I was, though, was uneasy and anxious.

"Well, enjoy your evening, children." She smiled and went into her own booth.

Something niggled at the back of my mind, but I lost it when Santini reached for my hand again.

"Don't," I said. "Please."

Something resembling regret danced across his face as he nodded.

"Let's go back here." He pointed to the area behind the booths where the electrical generators were stationed.

I had that heretic-shuffling-her-way-to-the-hangman's-tree stoop to my body again as I walked a little in front of him.

The alleyway behind the festival booths was dark enough so I knew no one could see us, but lit enough from the Christmas lights so we could see each other.

With the quiet whirr of the generator as white noise, Santini stopped. "Thanks for coming with me."

"I can't stay back here for long," I said, a little note of nerves breaking in my voice.

"Okay." He stood, rock still, staring down at me.

Something aside from the subtle hum of the

generator buzzed in the cold air around us as he looked at me. It took me a moment to recognize what it was, and when I did, I almost bolted.

I swear on a stack of Bibles and holding Nonna's rosary beads blessed by Pope Pius XII in my hands I could feel sexual tension palpating in the air.

There was no mistaking the charged energy bouncing between our bodies, though we were dressed head to toe in parkas, gloves, hats, and scarves.

I could smell it, pungent and spicy; feel it, hot and steamy; taste it, honeyed and sweet.

This is how animals must recognize their mates in the wild.

I was so glad it was dark because I knew my face looked as red as Mama's tomato sauce when it's coming to a soft boil.

Neither of us said a word. We just stared at one another. Even in the dark, I could make out the moisture flickering in his soulful eyes. His breath steamed into vapor with each expiration, a white puff of clear smoke veiling his face, and from the looks of it, he was breathing as hard and fast as I was.

My girlie parts suddenly got quite warm, the sensation not only shocking me, but exciting me as well.

I don't know how or why, but something pushed me from behind, actually shoved me forward with such force I landed in his outstretched embrace, arms circling and tightening around my waist.

"I—"

I couldn't speak because his arms around me felt like absolute heaven. I can honestly say being held by him was the most exciting sensation I've ever had in any guy's arms.

I took my time drifting my gaze up his neck, across his hard-as-concrete jawline, to his lips. From there it was a quick hop up to his eyes. And, *Holy Mother*, those eyes.

"Gia."

I took a deep breath and then sighed it out.

"Angels singing." I wasn't at all sure I'd said the words aloud.

"What?"

I swallowed, trapped in his stare. "When you say my name, I swear I hear angels singing."

"You're the angel," he whispered. In the next breath, his lips slid across mine.

He may have sounded and looked like a god, but he kissed like Lucifer himself, all heat and fire blasting from every movement of his mouth across mine. When his tongue slipped past my lips, he skimmed his hands down to my butt and pressed me as close as two people could get completely garbed in artic wear.

I heard someone moan, deep and throaty. In a heartbeat, I realized it was me.

Horrified, I yanked myself back with such force, I almost fell. Santini was quick, though, and reached out to save me.

"Stop. Let me go."

My hand flew to my mouth, my lips burning with the taste of him.

He started to say something, but I cut him off. "No. I can't do this. *You* can't do this. You're a priest—"

"No, I'm not."

"Well, not ordained, yet," I said, shaking my head, "but almost, so it's the same thing. Don't argue semantics with me."

"Gia." He took a deep breath in and shook his head. "I'm not a priest. Ordained, soon to be, or in any other way."

He looked so sincere, I stopped for a moment and just stared at him.

"Yes, you are."

"No, sweetheart. I'm not."

Not a priest? Yes, he was...wasn't he?

The little niggle jerking at me a moment ago tugged firm and rough in my head.

I nailed him with a hard-eyed stare. "Why did Sister Agnes call you Timothy?"

"Because it's my name." He cocked his head and shrugged. "Timothy Santini."

"I know that." I flipped my hand in the air like Mama does when she thinks you're being thick-headed and stupid. "But she didn't say 'Father Timothy.' "

"Correct, because, like I've been trying to tell you, I'm not a priest. I'm—"

"T? What are you doing back here?"

I turned my head to the voice. It was so familiar I had to blink twice before my brain registered the person standing behind Santini.

Clad in priestly black from head to toe, save for the weird green skullcap and gloves, stood...Santini. Another one.

Gesu. Two of them?

"What...who..." Those were the last two words I remember saying before the world went black in front of me.

Chapter Ten

"She's coming around. Her eyelids are fluttering." Chloe's voice sounded far, far away. "Come on, Gia. Wake up."

When I pried my eyes open, the first thing I realized was I was flat on my back on the ground, something warm and soft underneath me.

The second thing was that I was surrounded by people, like when Dorothy woke up in her own bed at the end of *The Wizard of Oz*. Chloe, Sister Agnes, and two, identical Tim Santinis, one of whom was holding my hand and rubbing my knuckles in a worried death grip.

A quick roll of my eyes told me I was in the back of our booth.

"Are you okay?" the Tim holding my hand asked, concern draping his face.

"I'm confused." He held on to me while I stood up. "What happened?"

"You fainted," Chloe told me, her arms folded across her chest. "You're lucky, too. Tim caught you before you hit your head on the ground."

I looked at the Tim holding my hand and then to the other Tim standing next to him, a duplicate look of concern on his face.

In an instant, the proverbial dawn broke.

"Twins?" My gaze shot back and forth between the

two of them.

"Identical," the other Tim said.

"You're Father Tim?" I asked the one cloaked in the cassock.

"No, I'm Thomas. He's Tim." He cocked his thumb at the guy holding my hand and grinned.

I looked up at him. "You're not a priest?"

"Not a priest." He shook his head and grinned exactly like the guy standing next to him. "Not even close. I manage a restaurant downtown."

"But I thought—"

"I know what you thought," Tim the non-priest said. "It's what everyone thinks until they see us side by side."

"We're monozygotic twins," the real Fr. Santini said. "Identical. Our mom's had three sets, us and two sets of girls."

"Dinner at your house must be fun," Chloe said, her lips lifting. "Or confusing as all hell. Sorry, Father. I didn't mean that the way it came out."

"No worries," Fr. Santini, the real one, told her.

"Most people can never tell us apart," Tim said. He glanced over at his brother, and his adorable grin grew. This grin, *his*, had my insides twitching.

"It'll be a whole lot easier now since your wardrobe is so telling."

They both laughed, high-fived, and grinned at me.

Twins. *Holy Mother of God.*

"Well, now, everything is fine here," Sister Agnes said, "so I'd better be getting back to my booth. The crowd is getting bigger."

"I need to go, too," Fr. Tom said. To his brother— *Gesu, his brother*—he added, "Call Mom. She wants to talk about Christmas Eve."

Chloe's attention was diverted by a couple of women who stopped to buy sauce, so it was just me and Tim, the non-priest, left.

"You're really not a priest?" I asked.

"Like I said, not even close."

My head screamed *yippie* and my heart went *zing*.

"Why did you think I was?"

I explained about setup day. "When Mama pointed to where you were standing, I thought you were the new guy. You were dressed all in clergy black, and I didn't see anyone else around I didn't recognize."

"Tom recruited me into helping, but a little while after we got here, Fr. Mario called him back to the rectory for something. And the reason I was all in black is because I was heading to work as soon as I was done."

"You manage a restaurant, you said?"

"Yeah. And before you ask, total black is the uniform."

It was easy to see how I'd made the mistake in his identity.

"I know Tom told everyone about our family during his first homily. Three sets of twins makes for a good introduction story. I'm surprised you didn't make the connection then."

I groaned out loud and rolled my eyes. "I would have if I'd heard it." I explained about Arianna's needing a diaper change. "By the time I got back upstairs, Communion had started, so I never heard what he said."

His sigh was loud and long. "When you ran away from me in the bakery, I couldn't figure out what the heck was wrong. After working together at the setup, it seemed we got along pretty good. There was something there, between us. I wanted to ask you out, was just about to suggest going for coffee when I got called away before I could."

"All those questions about sacraments and marriage," I said, remembering the conversation in full detail. "You were, what? Trying to find out if I was seeing anyone?"

"Yup. When you said you weren't, it told me I had a shot. But like I said, I had to leave. There was a crisis at the restaurant. There's always a crisis at the restaurant."

He rolled his eyes, and we both laughed.

"I was thinking about you nonstop that day. I don't even remember what the crisis was. I just knew I really wanted to see you again. When I saw you at Pontevecchio's, I couldn't believe my luck. But then, just when I was going to ask to see you again, you bolted."

I lowered my head in shame.

"I was convinced I'd misread the signs between us. Convinced you didn't, I don't know, like me."

"No." I shook my head. "The problem was I liked you too much."

It was his turn to nod. "I was all set to just try and put you out of my mind when I got the surprise of my life and saw you sitting on that park bench."

"It was a surprise, all right."

His eyes went all soft, his lids heavy, and I could tell he was remembering what happened between us in the park the same way I was.

"When you kissed me, well, all I could think was I was going straight to hell for having corrupted a priest."

He grinned again. "I tried to talk to you about it. I wanted to know why you kept running away from me. I didn't know what was wrong. I know kissing a total stranger like that was, well, not *usual*. But Gia"—he pulled me in closer—"I truly couldn't help myself. It was like someone pushed me from behind, straight into you. Once there, I didn't want to let you go."

I told him I'd gotten the same sensation.

"You have no idea what this past week has been like for me. Thinking I was going to hell one minute and not minding at all the next. Plus, I was as confused and mad as all get out every time your brother pretended not to know me. It's plain now, he didn't."

I gave him a quick rundown on the times I'd run into his brother and how angry I'd been when Tom, the real Fr. Santini, gave no indication we'd not only met but had been involved in a public make-out fest.

Tim stared down at me for a moment, his lips curving at the corners, making my toes curl again.

"Gia."

It was then I realized he was still holding my hand, had been the entire time. And just like before, it felt so right.

"So," he said, tugging me even closer until we were standing toe to toe, touching knee to knee. I had to lean back to see him clearly, and when I did, he slipped his hands around my waist. "About asking you out."

I smiled.

"Now that you know it's not—how did you put it?—*forbidden* for us to see one another?"

I squinched up my face, embarrassed at being so dramatic.

"How about dinner?"

"When?"

He laughed. "Right now seems good to me. What do you say?"

Gazing up at his grinning face, seeing the laughter and something more dancing in his eyes, I nodded.

"I just need to tell Chloe I'm leaving."

"No, you don't," she called out from the front of the booth. She snuck her head around the partition, smiled, and added, "Go. Please. Now. All these pheromones shooting off you two are making me miss my husband. Leave. *Tu vai.* Go!"

> *How to be a Good Italian, Lesson Eight:*
> *When you're told to leave, do it.*
> *No questions asked, no arguments.*

Without another word, hand in hand, we did.

****

So...

The night before Christmas Eve is usually the busiest one of the St. Rita's Festival. A year later, this still proved true.

Mama, Daddy, and I were all working, the family sauce flying off the shelves. This year, though, I had the added bonus of having my boyfriend of a year helping out as well.

From our first dinner date, Tim and I had been inseparable.

This was the first relationship I'd ever been in where everyone in my family, including a usually disapproving Nonna, liked the boy.

Tim was the best guy I knew. Truly. He worked hard, long hours at the restaurant, which had just expanded; he visited his parents every week, spoke to his siblings frequently, and treated me like what my father calls "an Italian princess."

We'd had a busy year together. I'd passed my licensing exams and had been recruited by the same firm where Tim's cousin Rocco worked, after he'd put in a good word for me.

I still lived at home, but since Tim had his own place downtown, more often than not I just stayed with him on the nights and days we were able to see one another.

Miraculously, my parents never said a word about the arrangements, and Nonna never threw a *malocchio* our way. Both of those very telling occurrences.

At nine p.m., the festival closed, and we started to pack up the unsold jars.

"I've only got a couple quarts left," Mama said.

Daddy kissed her on the cheek. "Everybody loves your sauce, Frankie."

"Gia and me can finish up," Tim told my parents. "Why don't you two head on home?"

A strange look passed between him and my dad, and then Mama nodded, a small smile on her lips.

They each kissed me, told me they loved me, and they'd see me at home. Before leaving, Mama pulled me into one of her bone-crushing hugs and Daddy looked like he had tears in his eyes when he hugged me, too.

"Okay, that was weird," I said when they'd gone.

"What was?" Tim circled his hands around my waist and pulled me into his arms. He dropped a kiss on my nose, then nuzzled it.

I swear to the Holy Virgin, my thighs started to vibrate.

"They're gonna see me in ten minutes, but from the way they acted, you'd think I was never coming home again."

Tim shook his head and pulled me in closer. "Not never," he said. "Just not as frequently."

Now I was really confused. "What?"

He pulled back, keeping me at arm's length. I don't ever think I've seen such a serious look on his face in all the time I've known him.

"Gia."

"Every time," I whispered, staring up at him. "Every time you say my name, I swear it sounds like angels singing to me."

He trailed a finger down my cheek and across my jaw. Taking a step back, still staring at me, he reached into his vest pocket and pulled out something I couldn't see. Whatever it was, it was small, because he fisted it in his hand.

He took my hand in his and—*Holy Mother of God*—got down on one knee.

"Since we met under these lights a year ago"—he pointed his chin to the top of the booth—"I figured this was the best place to do this."

"Tim?" I could barely whisper his name.

His smile bent into a crooked line, his brow folding together in the middle. "I don't know if you can understand this, but when we met last year, from the very first hour we were together, I knew this is what I wanted. That you were what I wanted. In my life. Forever."

"*Tim.*" Tears burned my eyes.

"My father always told us boys we'd know the girl we were meant to spend a lifetime with in a heartbeat of meeting her. I never believed it. I didn't think it was possible. Then, I met you."

He unfisted his hand and held up a ring between his thumb and index finger.

No, not a ring: a boulder. The thing was huge. The Christmas lights surrounding the booth bounced off it, making the area around us look like bright daylight.

"Tim!"

"And I knew what my father told us was true."

I couldn't stop the tears from water-falling down my face.

"Gia Gabriella Bernadetta San Valentino." He grinned, and I laughed through the tears.

Why did I have such a long name?

"I can't think of a future that doesn't have you in it. I've loved you from the moment I first saw you, and I promise I will never stop. I couldn't. I want a life with you, Gia. Children. A big house filled with them. As many as you want. But I want you most. Forever. Will you marry me? Will you make that life with me?"

How to be a Good Italian, Lesson Nine:
When the love of your life asks you to marry him,
say yes.

So I did.

A preview of Peggy Jaeger's

3 Wishes

by

Peggy Jaeger

A Candy Hearts Romance

"I'm culling," my mother said. With a snap of her wrist she sent another two-hundred-dollar silk shirt into a black plastic trash bag situated next to her bed. "I'm donating this stuff to the St. Benedict's yard sale. I filled a box of stuff I found in the attic belonging to you, too. It's on the dining room table. Go through it."

"Mama, why are you getting rid of all Daddy's clothes? Doesn't he need them?" I watched two pair of tailored black trousers fly from hangers and land squarely in the center of the bag.

"If he wanted them he should have taken them when he left with the bottled blonde *puttana.*"

I ducked as a hand-woven Italian-made leather belt went sailing past me, the buckle barely missing my left eye.

"Delphina's not a whore, Mama."

"No? What do you call a woman who steals a man from his family? His obligations? His devoted wife? A nun, maybe?"

She tore another shirt from a hanger with such force it pulled apart at the seams, rending into two jagged pieces of fabric. A feral grin crossed her pink glossed lips as she examined her handiwork.

"A mistake?" I ventured.

"*Puttana.*"

I knew there was no calming her down at this point. Ever since my father walked out of the home he'd shared with my mother for the past forty years to move in with his much younger, pregnant girlfriend, my mother had been on a tear.

"I'll go check on the box of things you left for me," I said, backing out of the room. I wanted to be alert for any more flying and potentially dangerous items coming my way. The near miss with the belt had stopped my heart cold.

Downstairs, in the dining room, where we'd eaten as a family for as long as I could remember until daddy's exodus, I saw the aforementioned box. It was an old-fashioned banker's box, plain brown paper bag finish on the outside, with a removable top.

From overhead I heard a small crash followed by Mama's loud "daughter-of-a-whore" litany in Italian. I ignored her, took the top off the box, and was immediately sent back in time to my eighth birthday.

Aladdin was the box office favorite at the time, and I'd asked for a genie-themed celebration, which included a visit to the movie with six of my closest friends, and a request for a real live genie to come to the house. Since I was the only girl back then, with four brothers ahead of me, I was used to being a wee bit spoiled. Okay, more than a wee bit. Until my sister came along a year later, and vaulted me out of the baby of the family position.

My birthday happens to fall on one of the busiest days of the year—Valentine's Day—and I know my parents had a hard time hiring a genie to come work my party. My Uncle Sonny knew a guy, who knew a guy, who ran a talent agency, though. Unfortunately, all the out-of-work actors employed at *Skippy Goldstein's Star Emporium* were booked for live appearances. *Cupids* poised to deliver candy grams; *Little Devils* set to bring naughty lingerie gifts and boxes of confections to wives, girlfriends, and mistresses. Skippy told Uncle Sonny he should have booked way in advance, to which, the family story goes, Uncle Sonny lifted Skippy out of his chair by his ugly skinny necktie and told him he'd better come up with a genie—and fast—or his relatives were going to have to dig through the Meadowlands marshes to recover his body.

Uncle Sonny's an intense guy.

An hour after the movie ended and we were all back at my house, the front door bell rang. When I answered it, there stood a tall, live genie, complete with four-inch turban, parachute pants a rapper would have envied, and genie slippers. You know, the ones that curl up at the toes and point upward? Way cool to an eight-year-old. Unfortunately, my genie was nothing like the one in the movie. First of all, he had a pasty white complexion, not a Caribbean blue one, was lanky and undernourished, not buff and solid, and he didn't speak with the rapid-fire hilarious staccato of the cartoon character but with a nasal Long Island twang which made him sound like he had the worst cold ever.

Ever.

Genie was a certifiable dud. But mama's goodie bags were a huge hit. Since my birthday is the day of the year overflowing with chocolates and candy of all kinds, she'd filled the treat bags to the brim with one sugared confection after another. My favorite was, and still is to this day, the little box of Candy Sweethearts with the cute sayings on them. While all the giggling girls around me were consuming their sweets as if it was going to be the last thing they ever ate on earth, I was hell bent on saving my Candy Hearts until after the party.

When everyone had gone, I raced up to my room, tore open the box, and dumped the contents onto my bed.

Every heart had a different saying stamped on it. From *I luv u* to *b mine* to *kiss me,* each candy bid the eater a sweet request. But my favorite one, the one that gave me a little woo-woo feeling when I found it, was the one labeled *3 Wishes.* The reason for my woo-woo-ness was because during his shtick, my pasty, pseudo genie had told me the following: "In honor of your birthday, Chloe, I grant you three wishes. Think hard and long about them before you tell me what they are." He'd tried to say it in a really theatrical, booming timbre, but it came out sounding as if he'd spent a night smoking and drinking at our neighborhood bar, Delvecchio's. Before I could tell him what my wishes were, my cousin, Tillie, gagged and threw up the orange ade Mama had served with lunch. Unfortunately, she aimed most of it for my genie's cool slippers. He screamed out a big girly "*yuk*" and then disappeared into the kitchen with Mama, where she tried her best to de-puke the shoes.

My Aunt Gracie was left to oversee the rest of the party.

Alone now, I tried to figure out which three wishes I wanted most. At eight it was pretty simple: I wanted world peace, no homework ever again, and to grow up and marry the man of my dreams. I'd actually written those three down on a piece of notebook paper and scotch-taped the individual candy to the bottom of the page. The tape was old and yellowed from the twenty-plus years it had held the Sweetheart in place. The candy's color itself was faded, but intact. A little heart-shaped pink confection with the words impressed onto it in a deep red.

I reached into the banker's box again and found my old diary, where I'd written my dreams and desires from the age of ten until sixteen. I'd stopped writing things down then because my little sister, fondly and forevermore called *Snoop,* had begun reading my entries to everyone. As I slipped the broken lock open, an errant page fell out and drifted down to the tabletop. I grabbed it and saw the date: my fifteenth birthday. As I had for every birthday since my eighth, I'd written down three wishes. All of them had to do with a guy. My dream guy. I'd wished he'd have one blue eye and one green, just like I had, so I wouldn't be the only freak I knew, he'd be a healer (I was big on watching reruns of old television shows like Marcus Welby, M.D. and E.R. at this age), and he'd fall in love with me in an instant.

Hey, I was fifteen.

Another crash from upstairs and then a stream of cursing in Italian had me shoving everything back into the box. When I got to the front door, the box in my arms, I called out, "*Ciao*, Mama. I'm leaving."

"If you see your father," she yelled back, "tell him he needs a new wardrobe."

****

"She's really pissed," I told Snoop the next afternoon while I tempered chocolate over a low-flamed double boiler. My sister was seated at the end of my shop kitchen counter, sampling the newest creation I'd concocted the night before, an Oreo cookie dipped in white chocolate and drizzled with caramel.

Did I mention I'm a chocolatier? My shop is called *Caramelle di Chloe,* roughly translated as Chloe's

Candy. In addition to my retail business, I cater all sorts of events: bachelorette parties complete with naughty anatomically correct chocolates, baby showers, anniversaries, and even weddings. I've been written up twice in national newspaper reviews, and my business is a solid, financially successful one. Recently, I'd begun to dream of expanding.

"*Dio mio*, Chloe. This is insane." My sister's beautiful blue eyes rolled back in her head as she licked her lips and savored the candy-cookie. "This is gonna be a major seller."

I smiled, pleased. I'd thought so too, but it was nice hearing it from someone else.

"So, are you going to tell Daddy about his clothes?" she asked, reaching for another sample.

"Not in this lifetime."

The chocolate was perfect, so I turned off the stovetop flame and dumped the gooey confection onto my marble countertop. Valentine's Day was a mere week away, and I had to get ready for the onslaught. While I smoothed the warm caramel from one end of the marble to the other and began rolling it between my gloved fingers into bite-sized nibbles of deliciousness, I told Snoop, whose real name is Gia, about the banker's box.

"She gave me one, too." Gia licked her fingers. "It was filled with stuff I don't even remember owning."

I mentioned the diaries and the candy Sweethearts in mine.

"Those are still your favorite." Gia grinned. "You work with the most delicious ingredients on the planet and you still love those little candies best."

"I know." Every year I featured candy Sweethearts

in some of my Valentine's Day offerings. I'd decorate cakes and cupcakes with them, fill bags tied with pink or red ribbons with them, add them to lollipop sticks, chocolate pretzel sticks, anything I could think of.

"Do you have any special plans for your big birthday?" she asked.

"Same ones I have every year. I'll be here, selling my yummy wares to the last-minute procrastinators, then home to a meal made by Mama."

Gia rolled her beautiful blue eyes again, and this time it wasn't because she was enraptured with my candy-cookie creation. "Just once, can't you let your staff run the shop?"

"Snoop, you know next to Easter, it's my busiest time of the year. I can pull in almost a quarter of my yearly earnings in the week leading up to Valentine's Day. That's not chump change."

"No, but it does happen to be a special day for you, as well. You should be celebrating. Not working."

We'd had this discussion any number of times over the years since I'd opened my shop at twenty-three, financed with a no-interest loan from my Uncle Sonny, the genie-procurer. I was almost thirty now, and the conversation was getting tiresome.

"You should be out with some hot guy who's all into you, at a club, having the time of your life. Not stuck behind a counter or in a kitchen, slaving away."

I let her drone on because, really, I'd heard this too many times before.

Anyway, there was no hot guy in the background, foreground, or any other ground dying to take me out on my birthday or any other day. Unlike Gia, who'd inherited our mother's genetics: small-boned, blonde-haired, and blue-eyed northern Italian features, I'd been blessed with my father's Sicilian DNA: average height, black hair, and prone to hairiness (I had to shave my legs every time I showered), with a tendency to chubbiness if I didn't watch myself, and the already noted one blue eye, one green.

Gia had hot guys beating down my parents' door to get to her. I did not.

The last guy I'd gone out with was a dinner date set up courtesy of my Aunt Gracie. He'd been a wise-guy wannabe with old world theories on women, namely the barefoot-and-pregnant kind. He'd picked out the names of our first six children before the tiramisu was served.

The guy before him told me I was married to my shop when I wouldn't devote every minute of spare time I had—which is not a lot—to him.

The one before him liked my candy confections more than me.

Face it; at a week shy of thirty, my dreams of happily ever after were starting to dwindle into the cold reality of perpetual singledom.

Later on, in my apartment over my shop, I dragged out the banker's box again and pawed through the rest of the contents Mama had shoved in there. But I kept coming back to the wish list I'd written at fifteen.

The funny thing was, I still wanted those three wishes even now at almost twice the age I'd been when I'd first written them. I knew the blue eye/green eye thing was probably never going to materialize. I'd grown to be comfortable with my weird eye status over the years. It was one of the first things people noticed about me, and the comments were usually positive and inquisitive, not hurtful and mean-spirited as they'd been during childhood.

The healer request could potentially happen. My shop is in a busy neighborhood surrounded by hospitals, medical buildings, and nursing homes. It wasn't too out of the ballpark to think I might meet a doctor, or a physical therapist, or anyone connected with the healing arts. The last wish—the one where the guy fell in love with me in an instant—was a total pipe dream, I knew. Love at first sight just doesn't happen in real life. Not in my world, anyway.

A word about the author...

Peggy Jaeger writes about strong women, the families who support them, and the men who can't live without them. When she isn't writing, you can find her either painting, crafting, or cooking. She loves to hear from readers on her website: PeggyJaeger.com and on her Facebook page:

http://peggyjaeger.com
https://www.facebook.com/pages/Peggy-Jaeger-Author/825914814095072?ref=bookmarks